For the Love of Food

A Sequel to Fried Rice

Leah Hermann

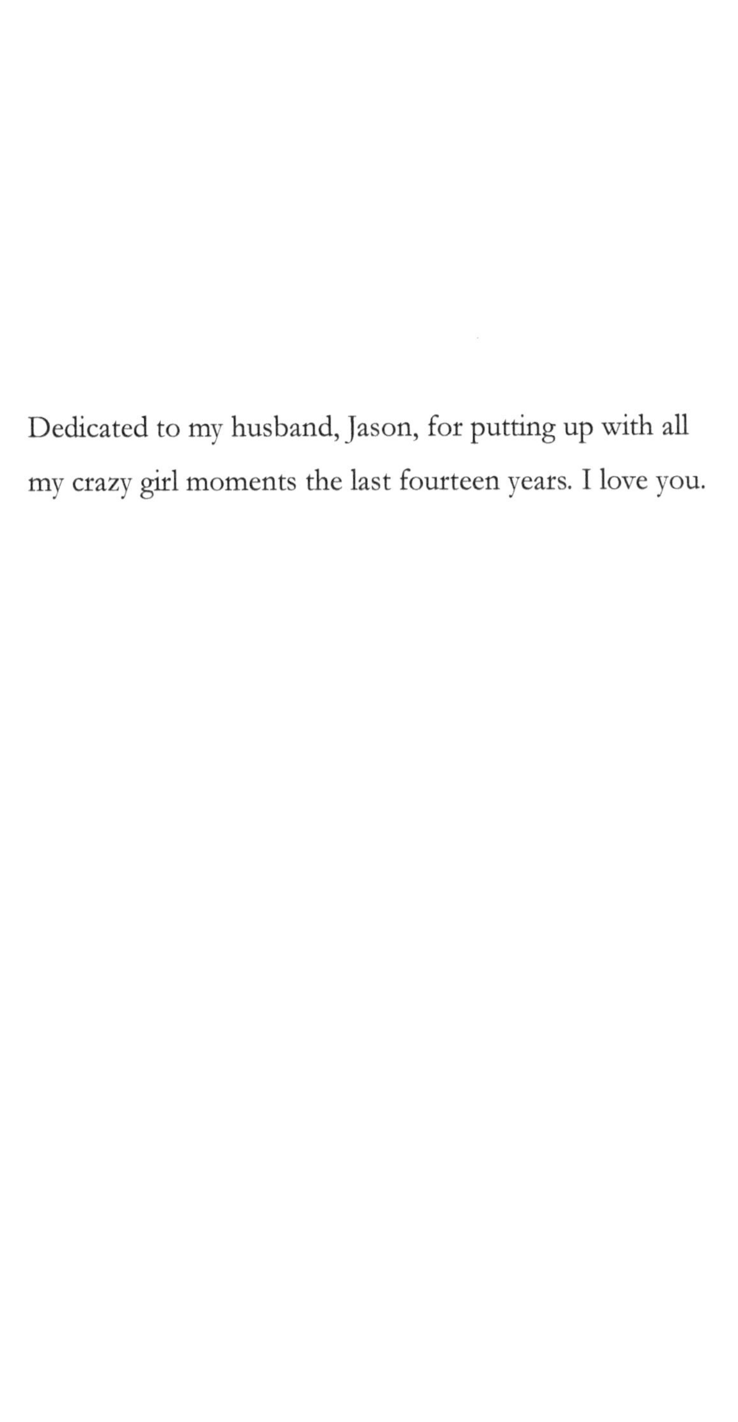

Dedicated to my husband, Jason, for putting up with all my crazy girl moments the last fourteen years. I love you.

Acknowledgments

Thank you to all my beta and proofreaders who took the time out of their busy schedules to help with my novel. I appreciate every one of you. Especially my brother, Chad, who forced himself to read all the "adult scenes" in both my Fried Rice manuscript as well as this one.

Chi Hom, what can I say? You killed it again! I am so thankful for your creative mind. Any author would be lucky to hire you to work your magic. I can't wait to see what else you come up with in the future.

Auntie Barbara, thank you for showing me endless support. I am blessed to have an auntie like you—one who hopes to see me excel at anything and everything I do. You are the best.

Special thanks to my editor, Liane Larocque. You were such a pleasure to work with. It's obvious you care deeply about your clients, and I can tell you want every writer you come in contact with to succeed. I'm appreciative of everything you've done to help make my novel better. I can't wait to work with you again.

Chapter One

V-Day

My pruney hand squeaks loudly against Brian's bathroom mirror as I wipe away the steam that has collected from my morning shower. I adjust the towel around my body and tuck it under my arm. My reflection stares back at me, and I try to guess what Brian has planned for our first Valentine's Day as a couple. As I run my brush through my damp hair, my mind begins to wander.

I imagine myself lying naked on Brian's bed that has hundreds of flower petals scattered over it. Brian lathers my body with lavender oil. His hands begin their journey as I inhale the scents of candles that are lit around the room. Brian whispers sweet nothings into my ear, and then he fully satisfies me like one of those girls in a sexy romance movie.

I sigh and decide to make more realistic guesses. There's a good chance Brian might order us a heart-shaped pizza for lunch, like the ones I've seen advertised on TV. He probably made plans to take us to the zoo. We haven't gone in a while. Maybe Brian will want to—

"Good morning, beautiful," Brian says while hugging me from behind and places his chin on top of my head. "I'm excited to spend Valentine's Day with you."

"I'm excited too," I say and set my brush down on the vanity. I turn and face Brian. He places his hands on my hips, and I look into his eyes—his gorgeous dark eyes that still draw me in every time, even after six months. "I feel like you haven't had one holiday off since we've been together," I mention.

"Yeah, I know. It's one of the perks of my demanding job," Brian jokes.

Brian's eyes are fixated below my neck, and I can tell he is imagining my naked body hidden underneath the towel. "But you know… we can start celebrating now to make up for all the other holidays I've missed," he says in a lowered voice—attempting to entice me. Brian's hands creep upward in hopes of removing my towel, which is wrapped against my chest. He kisses my forehead once and then my lips.

I playfully push him away. "Not yet! I haven't brushed my teeth!" I yell while laughing. I squeeze the rim of the towel tighter between my arms.

"Oh, come on! You know I don't care about that," he says frustrated and tries to pull me in for another smooch.

"No means no!" I say, jokingly. I quickly turn back toward the vanity and reach for my toothbrush, but I am secretly hoping Brian makes another move. Playing hard to get always makes it more interesting.

"Fine, I won't kiss you on the mouth then," he says.

I watch Brian's reflection as he wraps his arms around my waist, pushes himself against me, and gently kisses the side of my neck. His lips send chills down my warm, post-showered body, and I allow him to tempt me.

Each kiss makes my knees weaker, and my eyes involuntarily start to close. I brace myself against the vanity. I am helpless, and I give in. The grasp on my toothbrush loosens and slides to the bottom of the sink. My inhibitions diminish. I allow my towel to drop onto the bathroom floor, and I let Brian treat me like his puppet. He turns me back around and continues to kiss me wildly. My hands can't help themselves—eagerly tugging at Brian's sweatpants.

Unfortunately, Brian pulls away and yells, "Man, come on!"

I giggle at his frustration. "My daughter always has the best timing," I say, sarcastically.

Genesis is awake and demanding to be attended to. Brian adjusts his pants. "To be continued," he says, pointing his finger at me.

I nod my head and smile. Brian gives me a peck on my cheek before he sulks out of the bathroom to take care of Genesis.

As I retrieve my lost toothbrush out of the sink, I think back to the first night I stayed over at Brian's.

"Shoot! I think I forgot to grab my toiletry bag," I told Brian as I dug through my overnight bag.

"You can use my toothbrush," he offered.

I looked at him shocked. "Wait… are you serious?"

"What?" He shrugged. "I don't care," he told me.

"That is *so* disgusting!" I replied.

You'd think I had just been forced to eat a jar full of olives if you had seen my face. Brian's generosity made me wonder if he and his exes shared the same toothbrush. I tried not to vomit thinking about it.

"Why? It's no big deal." Brian chuckled. "It's the same thing as kissing."

"Are you kidding me?" I wanted to convince him and explained, "It is not the same thing! You know cavities are contagious, don't you?"

"What are you even talking about, Eva?" he said through his laughter.

"It's true! Cavities are contagious. It's a cold-hard fact!" I said, frustrated. He reminded me of his sister who was *also* constantly laughing at me. "Seriously!" I yelled and shot him an evil glance.

"You are so weird!" he replied.

I rolled my eyes and crossed my arms. "You always say I'm weird." Brian was really annoying me.

"Aw, I know, but that's my favorite part about you. There's no one else in the world who could be as strange as you." Brian started to poke at my armpits—the one spot he knew I hated being touched.

I tried to fight back… but of course, I lost.

My opinion about this matter will never change, no matter how long I've been with Brian. Using your significant other's toothbrush is *definitely* not the same as kissing, and no person on the planet could convince me otherwise.

I hang up the bath towel and put on my normal shirt and pair of leggings. Then I walk into the kitchen where Brian is busy scrambling eggs in a pan for Genesis.

"More!" Genesis says from her highchair. "More!" she continues to scream. Genesis is telling Brian she cannot wait another minute for her breakfast.

I grab a banana from the fruit basket. "Here, baby girl," I say to her as I quickly unpeel the fruit and break it up into chunks to put onto her tray. "You have to be patient. Your breakfast is almost ready."

She aggressively shoves a piece of banana into her mouth. The hungry monster is soothed for the time being.

I notice Brian had dressed Genesis in the onesie he

gifted her on her first birthday. Her chubby baby rolls barely fit into her snug outfit. She has grown so fast over the last few months.

"Aw, you are Mommy's little love bug, aren't you?" I say and kiss Genesis on her cheek.

"I thought you'd like that," Brian says while sliding Genesis' eggs onto a plate to cool.

I take Genesis out of the kitchen to give Brian more room to prepare our breakfast. His condo is quite a bit smaller than Brandi's townhome, but it's still a nice place.

One of the highlights of Brian's condo is the two bedrooms. When Genesis and I began making it a habit to stay over on Brian's days off, he insisted we put a crib for Genesis in his spare room.

I remember asking Brian why he decided to purchase a two-bedroom condo instead of a one-bedroom. I tried to focus my thoughts on why he decided to purchase the condo in the first place—Clarissa and Brian were growing apart. This logic should have made me feel better, but it didn't, and my insecurities continued to get the best of me.

"Wow, I really like your place," I told Brian as he gave me a tour. "Your living room is actually pretty spacious. A lot bigger than you were describing."

"Yeah, I guess it will do just fine for movie nights with my girls," he said while grinning. "I also have two bedrooms. The last couple of months I was thinking about getting a roommate, but then I figured Genesis and you could..."

I smiled as Brian's thoughts trailed off. Actually, I wasn't really sure where he was going with the whole deciding not to get a roommate thing. Even if he wanted us to stay over, it wouldn't matter if someone else was renting the second room. I didn't think too much about it because like I mentioned previously—insecurities—and I began to assume the worst. Assumptions of Brian hoping to fill his condo with a family bombarded my logic, and I couldn't help but wonder what his plans had been with Clarissa.

"So… how come you decided to buy a two-bedroom condo and not a one-bedroom?" I asked.

I wanted to justify my crazy girl thoughts. I mean, it didn't make sense. If Brian was predicting Clarissa and him were going to go their separate ways, why buy a place big enough for a small family?

"You know… I thought it would be smart just in case I needed the spare room or something," Brian explained.

Such a vague answer, but I also knew my assumptions got me into trouble from time to time. So, I quit thinking like a jealous girlfriend... at least for the rest of the day.

I park Genesis' highchair on the end of the table and smile as Genesis tries to reach for the vase of crimson tulips Brian had bought for me. Her short baby arms barely reach past her tray.

Brian walks over to the table with full plates of food in his hands. "Breakfast is served," he says.

"Thank you," I say. "And thank you for the flowers."

Brian and I smile at one another, enjoying our morning together. "You're welcome," he replies. "How are your eggs?"

I slide the edge of my fork into one of the eggs, and the yolk oozes onto my fried potatoes. "Perfect as usual," I tell him.

The first night I stayed over at Brian's, he ended up surprising me the following morning. I was completely in shock when Brian cooked me breakfast for the very first time.

"I'm going to take care of breakfast today," he told me.

"Really?" I asked. "So, you are going to cook breakfast… or is this your way of telling me you want to order pizza?"

Brian laughed at my assumption. "No, I don't want pizza for breakfast. I want to *cook* for you and Genesis."

"Oh, okay. That sounds nice," I said, hesitantly.

"So, how do you like your eggs cooked?" he asked.

"Uh, I like mine over-medium," I replied.

"You got it!" Brian said, confidently.

I expected my eggs to be too runny—the whites

slimy and still clear, or even worse, overcooked and rubbery. I expected my bacon to be crunchy in the middle and raw on the ends. I assumed my pancakes to be made from a box and mediocre… but they weren't.

"What did you think?" Brian asked after I cleaned my plate.

"I have to admit… I wasn't too optimistic about you cooking me breakfast, but I'm so impressed!" I told him. "You didn't tell me you can cook."

"Yeah, don't get too excited. Breakfast is the extent of my talent," he replied. "I've been watching tutorials on the internet and have been practicing the last couple of weeks—sixteen days… three times each day, to be exact."

"Breakfast, lunch, and dinner?" I asked, surprised.

"Yeah, that's why I didn't cook myself eggs this morning," Brian chuckled.

"Oh, my gosh. Now it all makes sense."

"What makes sense?"

"I finally understand why your farts smelled so bad last week—like rotten eggs," I joked.

"Yup!" Brian responded, proudly.

"Why is it that guys are always so pleased by their disgusting bodily functions?"

Brian shrugged while grinning. "Does it make you love me any less?"

"Uh, yeah, kind of!" I said, sarcastically.

"Ouch, Eva." Brian placed his hands over his chest. "That really hurts," he joked. "You broke my heart with your mean words." Brian ran his finger down his cheek, imitating a tear falling and made the most unconvincing pouty face.

"Well, you know, your farts about broke my lungs." I continued to play along, "So, I guess we're even now."

We had a good laugh talking about Brian's egg farts, but if I was being honest, I hated when Brian had to let out gas. Lucky for him, it wasn't a make it or break it type of deal, but I decided if Brian ever tried to suffocate me under the blanket with his farts… I saw it happen during some movie one time, and they called it a Dutch oven, or something like that. Well, anyway, if Brian were to ever "Dutch oven" me, we're done! Okay… maybe not *done* but doing so will earn Brian a trip to the doghouse, for sure.

"Anyway, who knows, maybe I can hunt down a video that teaches me how to make sausage or even waffles if you're lucky!" Brian said, changing the subject.

"Seriously though, I can't believe you taught yourself how to make breakfast!" I said, enthusiastically.

I was really proud of him.

"I love how you always cook for me. You take such good care of me," he explained. "I want to be able to return the favor once in a while."

Ever since that morning, Brian has cooked breakfast for us whenever we stayed over. This is one of the ways Brian shows Genesis and me he cares for us. I can't argue with his gesture because I strongly believe a good meal is one of the best ways of exhibiting how much you love someone. After eating one of Brian's delicious breakfasts, my love tank is always overflowing.

"What are the plans for today?" I ask Brian, hoping to get every detail in advance.

I wait patiently for an answer as he chews his last bite of food. "Oh, nothing too crazy," he says. A smirk emerges across his face, and I try to decipher the meaning behind it.

"Hmm, all right… So, are we staying in or did you have something else planned?" I ask.

Brian is aware I hate not knowing what my surprises entail, and it drives me crazy being out of the loop.

"I only have plans for tonight, but it requires you to go to the spa."

"The spa?" I ask.

"I scheduled you an appointment to get a massage. It's later this afternoon," he says, finally relieving me from some of my anxiousness.

I can't deny it—I'm kind of bummed the hands massaging my body today aren't going to be Brian's.

As I drive back from the spa, relaxed and rejuvenated, I think about the gift I made for Brian. I hope he likes it, like, *really* likes it.

For the last three weeks, I have secretly been painting him a picture at Brandi's townhome. I attempted to copy a picture taken of the three of us at the zoo. I tried capturing each and every detail of Genesis sitting on Brian's shoulders and my arms wrapped around his waist. I did my best to emphasize the joy on our faces as we stood in the aviary, surrounded by vibrant birds perched on different varieties of plants and trees. Well… the joy I painted on my face was one hundred percent fabricated because I really didn't want to stand under the birds any longer than I had to. I looked uncomfortable and terrified in the photo.

I knock on the outside of the door to the condo. "Hold on a second! Just give me two more minutes!" Brian yells.

The sun is just about to go down. I rub the sides of my bare arms to create warmth, confirming that Californians really are true wimps when it comes to cold weather. In my defense, I'm still wearing only my leggings and shirt from earlier today.

"Okay..." I respond as I think about walking back down the stairs to sit in my car, so I can blast the heater. I wait a moment before urging Brian to hurry. "It's kind of cold out—"

Brian opens the door. "Sorry about that," he says and gives me a kiss as an apology while I walk through the door.

I stare at the bedsheet hanging from the ceiling. "Oh, my gosh!" I say, laughing. "You made a love fort?"

Genesis is standing underneath the tent-like structure and grabs a rose petal to put into her mouth. Just as I'm about to sprint over to Genesis to remove the choking hazard from her hand, Brian reassures me and says, "Don't worry. They're fake." Genesis yanks the synthetic petal out of her mouth, and her face scrunches up in disgust. She throws it down on the pillows, disappointed.

"I bought us dinner," Brian says while pointing to the balcony.

I see he had moved the small dining table outside. "You did?" My eyes become wide. "Where did you pick up dinner?" I ask, impatiently.

"Get a sweater on, and I'll grab some warmer clothes for Genesis," he instructs. I'm positive he didn't answer my question on purpose, allowing the anticipation to gnaw at my insides. I hurriedly follow his directions, so I can find out what's for dinner.

"Well, you *definitely* nailed it! Best Valentine's dinner ever!" I tell Brian.

Brian holds Genesis on his lap while we enjoy our dim sum. His balcony barely has room for the table and two chairs. It's a little cramped, to say the least, but the view makes up for the lack of space—the city lights sparkle in the night sky. The view is mesmerizing.

I cut up some of my rolled rice noodles that are filled with shrimp and place them on a small plate next to Brian's. Genesis tests the texture of the noodles with her fingertips, remembers it's something she loves to eat, and quickly shovels a piece into her mouth.

"Thank you for making sure I had an amazing Valentine's Day," I tell Brian and savor a bite of the fried turnip cake.

"So, you enjoyed your massage?" he asks.

"Yeah, it was nice. I'm glad you went with the Swedish massage and not one of those cupping treatments that gives you hickeys all over your body."

"Huh?" he asks, confused. "What are you talking about?"

"You know… those massages where the masseuse heats the inside of the glass cups—"

"Wait!" Brian shouts. "Is this some kind of fetish thing?"

"What?" I tilt my head in confusion. "No, Brian!" I yell.

"Oh, well, the way you were describing it…" Brian trails off. Obviously, I'm confusing him.

"Okay, whatever!" I try to give him a visual. I pretend to hold a glass cup upside down with one hand while putting a flame inside with the other as I attempt to explain how a cupping treatment works. "They put the fire inside the cup… thingy… so it pulls out all the oxygen, and then they put it over the person's skin. It's like a suction…"

Brian finishes chewing and says, "Hmm. I don't know, Eva. Still kind of sounds like a strange fetish thing to me."

"Brian!" I shout. "Get your mind out of the gutter!"

"I'm not the one talking about kinky suction stuff," he replies.

Brian smirks, and I can't tell if he's messing with me. I roll my eyes and reply, "Oh, never mind!" I give up trying to explain, not really sure *I* even know what I'm talking about at this point. Maybe it is some type of sexual thing for all I know—my parents always did a good job at sheltering me. Plus, Brian would probably start laughing at me again if I continued with my rambling. "So, anyway. Yes. I really enjoyed my massage. Thank you," I say and continue to stuff my face with more delicious food.

"I can't wait for you to open your present," he tells me as we finish up dinner.

I sit up straight. My forehead scrunches up, and I look at him, confused. "Um, okay, but I thought the massage and dinner were my presents," I say, thinking my painting might not suffice.

I pick up Genesis off Brian's lap and get her ready for bed. I read her a quick bedtime story—a flipbook about finding a dog who has a spot on its side, which is one of my favorites from my childhood. I lay Genesis down in her crib. "Happy Valentine's Day," I tell Genesis. "I love you more than anything." I grab the stuffed elephant I brought over from Brandi's place and tuck it under my daughter's arm. I give Genesis a kiss on the top of her head and gently brush her bangs away from her sleepy eyes. As Genesis falls asleep, I am finally able to pull out my wrapped painting from under the crib, which happened to be the best hiding spot I could come up with.

Brian just finished cleaning up dinner and is lying on his side under the Valentine's fort he constructed. Brian pats the floor beside him, and I sit down next to him. I lean back onto the ridiculous amounts of pillows and notice some chocolate-covered strawberries in a heart-shaped container.

"Wow! You really went all out today!" I shout. "Don't they charge, like, $15.00 at the store for these five strawberries dipped in chocolate, or something insane like that?"

"Yeah," Brian responds.

My eyes bulge from my skull. "Seriously?" I ask.

"Uh-huh, but you don't have to worry about how much money I spent. I actually got a good deal on these."

"They had a sale?"

"Nah, some random dude had a whole set-up in his car. Whatever I was smelling from his vehicle didn't smell like chocolate and strawberries, but the quality of the fruit didn't look half-bad. He only wanted a couple of bucks, and well… ya know, I figured you were worth it."

"Oh, my gosh, Brian. Just stop," I say and shove his shoulder.

Brian smiles at me. He's satisfied I'm happy, but I also think Brian's satisfied with his really dumb, fabricated story. Brian's a real jokester tonight.

I hand him the large present I made, and Brian begins to unwrap it. "I know it's not much," I say. "You did so many things for me today, and I hope that—"

"Oh, woah, Eva!" he says surprised as he looks at the painting. "This is really amazing. I can't believe you painted this! You did paint this, right?"

I nod my head. "Do you like it?" I ask.

"Yeah, it's great. You really need to sell your paintings on the side or something." Brian flatters me. "I bet there's a ton of people out there that would love to buy your paintings."

I shrug. "I don't know about that."

"Seriously, you should. You could even do the whole art fair thing. You'd be the first one to sell out," he says, still admiring my work. "I'm going to hang this up first thing tomorrow." Brian wraps his arm around my shoulder and lands a kiss on my cheek, and then he starts to chuckle to himself.

"Why are you laughing?" I ask.

"And now I will always remember that you have a fear of bird poop," Brian mentions.

Now I think it might've been a better idea to have chosen a different picture from our trip to the zoo.

"Okay, sweet, let's go see some birds," Brian said to

Genesis and me. He pushed the stroller in the direction of the oversized, dark green cage.

My pace slowed as we neared the aviary. "Uh, are you sure you don't want to go this way?" I pointed my arm in the opposite direction. "The signs say there are hippos in this—"

"Yeah, come on. Let's go through here first, and then we can go see the hippos after," Brian suggested.

"Well, I guess I can always go around the aviary and meet you guys on the other side," I replied.

"What are you talking about?" Brian said. "How come you don't want to see the birds?"

I shuffled my feet on the ground as we stood in front of the caged entrance. "Oh, sorry," I said to a large family. They looked annoyed as they maneuvered around the stroller Genesis was in. I waited for the family of five to fully enter the aviary before I quietly admitted, "I'm afraid the birds are going to poop on my head… or just on me… in general."

Brian laughed at me for an entire minute before he said, "Eva, the birds aren't going to crap on your head. You don't need to be so deathly afraid of bodily fluids."

"It's not *all* bodily fluids!" I shouted. A worker walking by glared at me before continuing on his way. I tried to speak quieter and said, "It's just *poop* that makes me uneasy."

"I think you will be fine. There's no need to worry," Brian said, trying to encourage me.

Talking about bird poop in front of the aviary made my anxiety worse. "It's a real fear, Brian," I tried to explain. "It's called… what is it called? Ah! I remember. It's called Coprophobia." I said this proudly at the time, but now that I think about it, I probably shouldn't have.

"Huh? *Crap*-rophobia?" Brian said, mocking me.

"Oh, shut it!" I said.

I angrily pushed the door open with the side of my fist and decided I would overcome my legit fear of being pooped on, temporarily. Brian's peer pressure mixed with his mockery persuaded me to briefly conquer my anxiety.

I shoot Brian a dirty look. "It happens! It's a real thing! People get pooped on all the time when they go into aviaries!" I laugh but know I have every right to fear bird poop.

"Sure, whatever you say. Here, now open mine," Brian says while handing me a tiny box he pulled from underneath one of the many pillows lining the love fort.

"Ooo, did you buy me jewelry?" I ask, trying to guess.

"No, not exactly," he says.

I continue to hold the box in the palm of my hand. "Ooo, I bet it's a—"

"Stop trying to guess and just open it," Brian says, annoyed.

I slowly pull the top off the box, and to my surprise, there's a key inside.

"What's this?" I ask, confused. "Well, I mean, I know what it is, but what's it to?"

Brian clears his throat, "Well, I, uh—" The last time I had seen Brian this unsure of himself was when he brought up his ex-girlfriend. "I was thinking… since Brandi and Max are going to be married in a few months, maybe, Genesis and you would want to move in with me?"

Brian nervously grins at me, but I'm not sure what to say. I look at Brian and again at the key in the box. "Um," I stutter, trying to stall while I think about my answer.

Max had already moved in with Brandi… and me last month. It did feel a little crowded in her townhome, and Genesis and I have been staying over at Brian's on his nights off, but I'm not sure if I am willing to take the next step in our relationship just yet.

Memories of Liam in our apartment start to cloud my brain. His hurtful words flow in and out of my head. Pictures of Liam leaving me and his daughter escape from the back of my mind and—

"So, what do you think?" Brian asks, hopeful.

"Uh, I don't know. You don't think it's too soon?" I ask, knowing Brian *obviously* doesn't think his request is premature.

"Hey, there's no rush," he tells me. Brian places his finger under my chin and tilts my head higher, which forces me to make eye contact. "Just keep the key. When you feel the time is right, I will be more than ready for you to move in with me."

I smile at him, and I am thankful he didn't pressure me into making a decision tonight. I pick up one of the chocolate-covered strawberries and hold it up to Brian's lips.

This is when I learned *food is a form of intimacy.*

As Brian takes a bite, I tell him, "You know, I actually have one other Valentine's gift for you." I grab the back of his neck and kiss him, long and hard.

"Oh! Okay… yeah, I like this gift," he says while pulling my T-shirt over my head.

I lean back against the pillows and look at him. I try to look serious and say, "You mean, you like this gift *more* than the painting that I spent countless hours on?"

"Yeah—uh, wait. This is a trick question," Brian says.

"No, it's really not," I reply, but I can't keep a straight face any longer.

I place my hands on Brian's chest and push him onto the pillows—forcing him to lie on his back. I hover over him and gaze into his eyes. "I love that you bought me my favorite food today," I tell him and begin to kiss his neck. "I love that you bought me some… questionable strawberries." I giggle and slide myself down lower. I impatiently lift Brian's shirt, and my lips linger on his rock-hard abs. "But most of all, I love you," I say in a sultry voice.

Brian sits upright, and my journey down his body abruptly comes to a halt. I sit up too and look at Brian, slightly disappointed he ended my journey down his perfect body. He brushes my hair away from my cheek and says, "And I love you, Eva. You are the best thing that has happened in my life."

I tackle Brian onto the pillows again, but he flips me over onto my back and finishes undressing me. I can feel Brian's chiseled torso on my stomach, and I envelop his broad shoulders in my hands. As my eyes roll to the back of my head, I imagine this is the same feeling addicts experience when pumping heroine through their veins. My mind succumbs to the euphoria being released into my body, and I drown in pure ecstasy.

Chapter Two

Cat Fight

"See, Mom, I told you, you would be seeing your granddaughter just as much," I say, handing Genesis to my mom. "You're only missing out on a couple days less a month." I take Genesis' lunch out of her baby bag and stick it in my parents' fridge.

"Yes, you were right, Hunny," she replies. "But I can never get enough time with my darling grandbaby." She pinches Genesis' cheek, and luckily my daughter doesn't mind how my mom shows her affection. "So, how is Liam doing these days?" my mom asks.

"Uh, probably a lot less lonely," I say. I become annoyed, thinking back to when I spoke to Liam over the phone. Just as promised, I called Liam up the day after he had gotten an eyeful of my scandalous panties on

Brandi's coffee table.

"So, what's going on?" I asked Liam.

"I've come to the conclusion that I would like Genesis to be a part of my life," he said, hesitantly. "I would love to take her a few days out of the month… on my days off."

I wasn't surprised that my assumptions turned out to be correct. "Oh, okay," I said, guarded.

"Do you think we could work something out?" Liam asked, hopeful.

There was a long pause while I sorted out my feelings. I was angry but also elated at the same time. Better late than never is typically the normal response in this situation, or at least I thought it was. I honestly couldn't help but feel uneasy about Liam's request.

Old but potent feelings started to resurface. Resentment began to spread throughout my body like harsh cancer that no longer laid dormant. I angrily grasped my phone in my hand as I thought back to the moment when my belly was just beginning to protrude over my hips. Days after, I realized my daughter would grow up without a father. I clenched my teeth tightly as I thought about the day my mom drove me to the hospital. I remembered the loneliness and pain I endured while giving birth to Genesis.

As I thought about the audiologist telling me my daughter had hearing loss, I forcefully shut my eyes in hopes of stopping more painful memories from presenting themselves.

It was no use. I felt the heartache I endured when I realized Genesis had special needs. I was back in the past, feeling helpless and alone.

As my grudge lingered, Liam continued to explain his reasoning for returning a year after his daughter's birth. "I bought my own place," he said.

"That's… nice," I responded because, at the time, I assumed Liam was bragging about purchasing a house on his own.

"I ended up adopting a tabby cat."

"All right…" I replied, wanting our conversation to end.

"She really has a great personality," he explained.

I thought Liam might be trying to create small talk or something. I thought he ought to be telling me how great a personality *his* daughter had instead.

"Cool," I responded.

"I just bought her one of those really nice scratching posts. It has a hideaway on top of the post and everything," Liam said.

He sounded like a crazy cat lady. "Uh, nice," I replied.

I heard Liam release his breath into the phone's speaker before he continued. "The house is just so empty. Even with a four-legged friend to keep me company."

Oh, now I understood. Liam wasn't tooting his own

horn after all. He was lonely. Well… poor Liam! I allowed my hate to fester a while longer.

"I thought it would be nice to have Genesis over," he mentioned. "I think we would have a nice time together."

I ended up telling Liam I understood and was happy he wanted to spend time with his daughter. The whole understanding part was a straight-up lie.

"Have Brian and Liam warmed up to one another yet?" my mom asks, nosily.

"No, not exactly," I tell her. "I've just been trying to keep them separated. I've been dropping and picking Genesis up at Liam's place, so he doesn't run into Brian at the condo again."

My mom's face looks sympathetic. "That's probably a good idea, Hunny," my mom tells me.

The first time Liam had dropped Genesis off at Brian's place, I thought I was going to have a front-row seat to an MMA cage fight—one of those fights where two crazy people go at it bare-knuckle style.

I remember watching a couple minutes of a gory fight when Liam decided to throw a watch party at our apartment. For most of the night, I locked myself in our room, but when I had no choice to walk past the living room, I couldn't help but glance at the TV. I cringed as I witnessed the worst moments of the fight—the losing guy's face was cut up and blood was gushing everywhere.

He looked like Carrie when she went to her prom and had pig's blood dumped all over her. So disgusting! I never understood Liam's choice in entertainment. I guess if I had to choose between watching a pervy adult cartoon or a bloody barbaric fight, I'd go with the adult cartoon.

Anyway, Liam returned Genesis with a huge bump on the top of her forehead.

"What happened?" I said panicked, grabbing Genesis from Liam's arms. "Aw, my baby girl, are you all right?" I kissed Genesis on her forehead beside her fresh bruise and looked at Liam, patiently waiting for an answer.

Before words could leave Liam's mouth, Brian stood up from the couch and walked over to Genesis and me. Brian gently rubbed his thumb over my daughter's black and blue lump.

At that moment, Liam reminded me of that one guy from X-Men—the one with the laser eyeglasses. I could never remember their names or the proper nerdy terminology, which always used to annoy the crap out of Liam. The point I'm trying to make is, Liam's glare was so intense *just* like that X-Men character's. I thought his eyes were going to burn right through Brian's skull.

"Uh, Liam… so, are you going to tell me what happened?" I asked concerned.

My words were barely able to snap Liam away from giving Brian the death stare, but eventually Liam finally took his focus off my boyfriend and turned his attention to me. "Yes, um, she fell after trying to stand up by herself," Liam explained.

I questioned Liam further. "*Okay…* but what did she hit her head on?"

Liam seemed like he didn't want to tell me the whole story. "She hit her head on my… fireplace," he admitted.

Brian inhaled deeply and his breath remained inside his lungs. His lips were shut tight.

I tried to be understanding to prevent an argument and said, "Hmm. All right, well I know—"

"Probably not the best idea to let her play around the fireplace, don't you think?" Brian interrupted—somewhat… calmly. Brian did a fairly good job at hiding his anger and frustration, but his tone still sounded a tidbit agitated.

Liam didn't like Brian butting in—or, speaking to him in general. "I didn't think she was going to fall and hit her head. It was an accident," Liam tried to explain, but unlike Brian, Liam didn't even attempt to suppress his anger.

"Did it happen today?" Brian asked, genuinely curious.

Liam looked like he was starting to become more offended by Brian's questions. I wasn't surprised. This wasn't the first time I had seen Liam in his hotheaded state.

Liam took a step toward Brian and angrily said, "Why does it matter when it happened?"

I thought I saw Liam's heels rise off the floor. He was pretty tall for a Chinese man, but not nearly as tall as Brian. I think Liam was trying to close the height gap for intimidation purposes, but I'm pretty sure it wasn't working. Liam just looked ridiculous, standing on his tippy toes.

"I'm just curious is all," Brian replied. "I know accidents happen, but if it happened recently, I will put some ice on it, which will help with the swelling." Liam inched a little closer to Brian's face. Brian wasn't having it and said, "But you gotta' back up, buddy. I'm not looking to get into a confrontation with you."

Brian was really killing Liam with kindness.

"I did put ice on it! I'm the one with the medical degree, not you," Liam told Brian, sharply. Liam's hands started to curl into fists. "You aren't Genesis' father. I am, and I'm not your buddy."

"Um, can we please stop now," I said, quietly. Liam didn't hear me, or I should say, he *chose* not to hear me.

Brian took a step back but didn't break eye contact with Liam. "Hey man, I'm not trying to tell you how to raise your daughter or anything—"

This was a hundred times worse than Brian and Ken at Genesis' birthday party. "Okay!" I yelled, stepping between the two of them. I dramatically pushed my hands on each of their chests to widen the space between them. I think my arms ended up recoiling back toward my body because neither of them moved—not even an inch.

I continued to try to ease the tension in the room. "It's not a big deal. I will put some ice on it… again," I said and quickly urged Liam out the door. Just before he turned his back to me, I quietly told him, "I know things happen, but please try to keep her away from the fireplace."

I shut the door behind Liam and saw Brian grabbing some ice from the freezer. "What's with you and the cocky guys with medical degrees?" Brian asked, annoyed.

I sighed and shook my head, "Honestly, I don't even know."

So, ever since that day, I had been keeping Liam and Brian away from one another.

"How have you and Dad been this last week?" I ask my mom.

"Oh, not too bad, Hunny, but your dad has been a stubborn ass lately," my mom explains. "No matter what I say or do, he still won't get a dang hearing test."

"I heard that!" my dad yells from the living room. "I told you I can hear just fine!"

I can't help but laugh. "Must be selective hearing," I say.

I close my eyes and breathe in the sweet aroma of barbecue pork that has filled the kitchen. "Ooo, are you making Char Siu?" I ask my mom. I don't wait for a response and anxiously open my parents' oven to see if my sense of smell is correct. Thankfully, it didn't deceive me. Charred, fatty strips of pork shoulder sizzle on top of a rack in the oven. I close the door and smile at my mom, knowing full well she will offer me some because food is love, and she loves her one and only daughter more than life itself.

My mom smiles at me warmly. "I will pack you up some to take with you when you come back from work," she says.

I would never say no to my mom's perfected Char Siu pork. "Thanks, Mom," I say and then give Genesis a peck on the cheek before heading to the cafe.

Chapter Three

Wedding Vibes

"Dude! Seriously? I shot that guy in the head, like, five times!" Max screams in frustration. Max is sitting on my couch bed and has been playing his video games for the last two hours—possibly longer.

Brandi shakes her head and rolls her eyes at her fiancé's life dilemmas. She grabs the large pile of invitations and loudly taps the bottom of the cards on the table to align them into one, neat stack.

"I have to get these sent out by tomorrow," Brandi tells me while gluing a tiny, silver bow onto an invitation. The last couple weeks Brandi has been in a frantic mood, trying to get everything in order for her wedding.

"I feel like three months is plenty of time for your guests to ask for time off and plan ahead," I reassure her.

"And we should be able to finish the invites before Genesis gets up from her nap. So, there's really no need to stress."

"Sure would be nice if Max would get off his stupid video game and come help us!" Brandi says loudly to her fiancé.

Max ignores her, partially because he has a headpiece on, but also because he is in the middle of an intense deathmatch. Max moves his controller back and forth and sometimes even around in circles. I'm pretty sure Max believes the unnecessary movements make him a better gamer, and I can't help but let out a little giggle.

"You know, I think I've heard a saying—a couple who games together stays together," I tell Brandi.

She looks at me and rolls her eyes again. "I told Max he needs to help with yardwork and taking out the trash, and if he does all those things then he is more than welcome to game as much as he wants, but no way will you ever catch me gaming. Ever."

"I guess that's a fair deal," I say and slide one of the invitations into an addressed envelope.

"So, anyway, how's it going with my brother? I feel like I barely see you anymore with my work schedule and you staying over at Brian's *all the time*," Brandi says.

"I don't stay over *all the time*, but yeah, I know. I wish I could see you more often too. Brian and I… well, you know, it's going really great," I tell her. "Oh, you just reminded me. I did forget to mention something. On

Valentine's Day, your brother gave me a key to his condo."

"I guess I could've seen that coming," Brandi says while smirking.

"Well, um, so he actually asked me to move in with him. Hence, the key," I explain.

"That little butthole! He is *obviously* trying to steal my personal chef!" Brandi jokes. "So, what did you tell him?"

"I told him I wasn't sure. I'm just nervous, you know."

Brandi nods her head.

"The thought of someone leaving me and Genesis again really freaks me out." I pause from my job of filling envelopes. "I know he's not Liam, but I can't help but have a little doubt in the back of my mind."

Brandi looks at me and briefly rubs the back of my shoulder. "I feel ya, girl," she says. "But like you said, Brian isn't Liam. Brian loves you and Genesis more than anything."

"Yeah, I know... I'm just being paranoid. You're probably right. I mean, Brian didn't pressure me for an answer or anything. I just feel bad because I still haven't given him an answer, and it's been a little over a month. Your brother really is so sweet. He hasn't asked me about it once since Valentine's Day. He's just… patiently waiting on me." I shoot Brandi a slanted smile.

"You will figure out what's best for you and Genesis," Brandi assures me. "Just focus on the invites.

The wedding invites are the most crucial right this moment! I didn't *actually* want to hear about your relationship drama with my brother," Brandi says, sarcastically. She winks at me and bumps the side of my arm with hers.

I shove a couple more invites into their envelopes and smile. "You know, I probably should cook us some lunch now. What do you think?" I ask Brandi.

"Oh, hells yes! Please!" she replies. Brandi looks at Max still gaming hard and walks over to him. She unforgivingly pulls off his microphone.

"No, no," Max squeals, still trying to finish what he started. "The match is just about over."

"It's okay Brandi. Max doesn't have to help me," I say. "I've got it under—"

"Max, get your butt in the kitchen and help Eva!" Brandi shouts and pulls Max off the couch. Max tosses the controller onto the couch, defeated. Brandi's hand slaps Max's rear end to corral him into the kitchen, and unfortunately, I think I witnessed his butt-cheek jiggle. So awkward.

Brandi sits back down to finish up the wedding invites, and Max joins me in the kitchen as my sous-chef.

"So, what can I help you with?" Max says as he washes his hands.

"Um, well, I thought we could have some steamed dumplings for lunch," I tell him.

"Mmm, mmm! Yes! That sounds phenomenal!" Max

responds, enthusiastically.

I place my container of pork filling I made the other day on the counter, as well as a bowl of egg wash and wonton wrappers, in the middle of Max and me.

"All right, so all you do is take a small spoonful of pork filling and use another spoon to slide it onto the wonton wrapper," I explain, instructing Max while I show him how to fill a dumpling. He copies me. Then, I brush the wrapper with egg wash and make small pleats, bringing the two sides together as one. "Okay, now your turn," I say.

Max's inexperienced hands begin making ununiformed pleats along the wonton wrapper. He looks like a little kid molding putty. "Uh, oh, nooo!" he yells. Max's wonton wrapper tears and the filling plops down onto the counter. Max hangs his head over in defeat. Brandi and I both laugh at poor, discouraged Max.

"It's fine. Just go ahead and put the filling on a new wrapper and try again," I tell him.

His dumpling skills remind me of when I was eleven during one of my mom's cooking lessons.

This is when I realized *food is a form of knowledge.*

"Mom, I can't do it," I told her after ruining my fourth dumpling in a row. I had the most exaggerated pouty expression plastered on my face.

"Sure, you can," she reassured me. My mom

positioned herself behind me, wrapped her arms around me, and placed her delicate hands on top of mine. She helped guide my uncoordinated fingers through each pleat, carefully and slowly. "See, I knew you could do it," my mom said.

I held the dumpling in my hand like a baby chick that had just hatched. I was so proud of myself.

"Ah, shoot!" Max screams after ruining another dumpling.

"Don't give up," I say. "I've been there. Just try and cup the dumpling underneath with your bottom fingers and take your time. Make each pleat *slowly* and *carefully*."

"All right, I got this," he says, taking a step away from the counter. Max shakes his arms and legs out like someone getting ready to get into a boxing ring. I start to laugh even harder, and I see Brandi roll her eyes for the third time today. "Okay, let's do this!" he says. Max tosses his ripped wrapper into the trash and begins again. "Third time is a charm, right?"

Max successfully closes the dumpling halfway, and I encourage him to keep going. "See, there you go. You're almost there!"

Max grins. "Brandi! I did it!" he says, excitedly showing her the completed dumpling.

This is when I realized *food is a form of accomplishment.*

"Great job!" she replies. Brandi begins clapping her

hands in the air, high above her head. "Before you know it, lunch will be ready in the next *decade*."

Max chuckles at her sarcasm and starts on the next dumpling.

"You're doing amazing," I tell him. It is nice to have a helper in the kitchen. "I can't wait for Genesis to be beside me, helping me with meals."

"Genesis will probably be a lot more help than I am," he says and then chuckles to himself.

"Trust me. You are a fast learner. I'm impressed."

"Thanks. So, I did hear you mention something about Brian asking you to move in with him," Max mentions.

"Oh, so you *can* hear us when you're gaming? All right, I will keep that in mind." We both laugh. "Yeah, I've really been considering it. I mean, you and Brandi are practically married. I don't want to intrude."

Max shakes his head. "You don't need to worry about that. If anything, I've been the intruder, stepping into your and Brandi's domain."

"Oh, please!" I shout.

"It's true," Max says. "I should be thanking you for putting up with me."

"You know you can stay with us as long as you want, Eva," Brandi chimes in.

"I know." I smile at her. "I really appreciate it, you guys."

"Maybe you can teach Max how to cook some more

meals, and then we won't starve to death when you decide to leave us," Brandi jokes.

"Yeah, I could learn!" Max says, proudly. Again, he happily displays his second completed dumpling. "I really appreciate you showing me how to fill these little guys. Maybe you can show me how to make the filling next time?"

"Of course, Max!" I say, enthralled he is interested in my cooking. I give Max a side hug. "I'd be more than happy to teach you."

"They say a way to a man's heart is through his stomach, but now I am convinced the way to Brandi's heart is through your cooking," Max says.

"Whatever, Max! You never cooked me shit while we were dating," Brandi says still joking around.

Max grins at her comment. He must love Brandi's blunt humor as much as I do.

"If I can keep cooking this good after you leave, Brandi will have a nice belly like mine," Max says, and he takes a moment to pat his stomach. "Then maybe, my friends and family will stop asking me how I managed to seduce such a beautiful lady like Brandi." Max walks over to his fiancé who is still sitting at the table and kisses her on the lips.

I think I see Brandi blush. "I'm the lucky one," Brandi says. "Plus, your belly *is* one of your best qualities. I will leave you in a heartbeat if it disappears and you get ripped. I'm dead serious," she says.

"Ooo, you think my sexy belly is my number one quality?" he asks Brandi. Now Max is rubbing his stomach with both of his hands and exaggeratedly rolling his upper body along with his arm motions.

"No, I said *one* of your best qualities. Not best," Brandi replies.

"Okay, so then what is my number one quality?" he asks.

"Well, your big—"

"Ah! Okay, that's enough of that!" I shout. Brandi leans over the table, laughing uncontrollably. Brandi has convinced herself she is a comedian.

Max has a big smile strewn across his face, but then he looks at me and chuckles uncomfortably. Now Max's face is bright red due to my presence and Brandi's raunchy humor.

I try to ease his embarrassment. "I love you, Max. I'm so glad Brandi found you," I say. "I'm also glad you are able to relate to our love of food. You are a perfect fit."

Chapter Four

Nobody's Maid

After Genesis and I have breakfast with Brian, I finish washing the dishes. I briefly watch Brian toss Genesis up in the air and then spin her around in circles.

"Woah, Genesis! You are going too fast!" Brian shouts as my daughter's laughter reverberates throughout the room. "You are such a little daredevil!"

I smile to myself and grab the cleaning supplies from underneath Brian's kitchen sink.

"You know you don't always have to clean my bathroom, Eva," Brian tells me as I walk toward the restroom.

I slide on my pair of yellow gloves I stored at Brian's condo. "It's fine. I don't mind," I reply.

He pauses from spinning and replies, "Well, I think

I… kind of mind."

"It's fine. I'm used to it," I respond.

"Used to it?" Brian asks, confused. "What, my sister makes you clean her townhome too? Cooking isn't enough?"

"No… I mean, I help her clean every now and then, but Brandi does plenty," I reply and think back to living with Liam.

"Liam, can you please try to put your whitey tighties in the hamper?" I asked, politely as I picked up his underwear off the floor.

"I can't hear you," he yelled from the living room.

I walked out of our bedroom. "Your whitey tighties were right beside the hamper again," I explained.

Liam took a minute to look away from the TV and shouted, "Babe! They are briefs. For the last time, call them briefs!"

I didn't think there was really a difference, but whatever. "Can you please make sure you put your… *briefs* inside the hamper?"

Liam ignored me and continued watching his dirty anime movie. I drowned my annoyance and grabbed the vacuum out of the closet, knowing full well Liam would tell me to vacuum when he wasn't watching his inappropriate adult cartoons.

My assumptions were correct. Just seconds after turning on the vacuum, Liam started to complain. "Babe!

Can't you wait fifteen more minutes?" he screamed over the suction sounds. I noticed Liam throwing his hands in the air, frustrated with my timing. Then he angrily grabbed the remote and turned the sound up twice as loud.

Liam constantly demanded a clean apartment, but on his time and his schedule. How dare I start cleaning the bathroom while he was in the shower or wash dishes when he was getting a snack. Why would I ever think washing the bedsheets was okay? How was I supposed to know Liam suddenly needed to take a nap? And more importantly, how come I wasn't able to get all the laundry done in a timely manner so Liam could wear his favorite pair of jeans?

Speaking of the universe revolving around Liam and my maid services—I also remember, one time, he told me his internship took priority over my job at the cafe. The fact that he was making more money than I was automatically made cleaning my second job. Liam was so confrontational and such a hothead. I tried my best to avoid arguments with him.

Word for word, Liam said, "I make the money around here, so you can help with the housework." During his internship, he really wasn't making *that* much more than I was.

I soon realized that "helping with the housework" meant doing *everything* around the apartment, but I didn't know any better and didn't contest Liam's demands. I thought it was kind of typical for a woman to maintain the home.

At a young age, my mom taught me how to wash, iron, and put away my own laundry. I remember whining as I was forced to fold my clothes into a neat stack. I frustratedly asked my mom why I had to help her.

"You need to know how to do these things for when you have a husband and a family to take care of," my mom told me. She continued to match my dad's pairs of socks and fold one over the other.

"Why doesn't Daddy help you with laundry and other stuff around the house?" I asked, thinking I could go and do fun things if my dad helped out instead.

My dad worked hard to make money, but he never assisted my mom with housework. Not once. Not ever.

My mom just smiled at me and changed the focus back onto my poor laundry skills. "Just keep at it, Hunny. You are almost done."

My shoulders slumped over. I pouted for a second and eventually picked up another article of clothing out of the basket. "Can I go and ride my bike after I'm done with laundry?" I asked, hopeful.

"I still need you to help me with the dishes. Then you can go and play," my mom said and patted me on the top of my head.

"Ugh! Mom!" I yelled, complaining.

She replied with a stern look.

"Fine," I said. Not that I really had any say in the matter.

"Like I said, you need to know these things for when you have a family," she reminded me.

I wasn't sure I believed her at this moment, but it turns out, the conversations I had with my mom carried over into my adulthood—especially the conversations like these ones. My mom instilled in me that housework is a woman's job in our culture. At times I wondered, if I managed to work my way up to a successful career… would I still be required to maintain the house by myself?

Brian put Genesis in the walker he had recently purchased for her, and she runs back and forth around his condo.

"Here, let me get it this time," Brian says.

He walks into the bathroom and reaches for the sponge and cleaning spray I hold in my hands. Brian looks determined like he won't take no for an answer.

I give him a kiss, pull off my gloves, and take Genesis out of her walker so she can get some legit practice walking. I sit down on the couch to keep an eye on my daughter. Genesis screams with pure excitement—enjoying her freedom.

I let out a sigh and think about how I tend to get nervous watching her try to walk too fast, anticipating the fall that comes shortly after. I am always relieved when Genesis pulls herself off the floor—strong and brave. I like to think I passed down those qualities to my daughter. She has become accustomed to falling and dusting herself off.

Chapter Five

Days with Daddy

Every other Sunday, I drop Genesis off at Liam's house. Genesis usually cries when she realizes I'm going to leave her with Liam—someone she's not as familiar with. Genesis' insecurities make it hard for me to say goodbye to her, or maybe it's my insecurities that make it difficult. Either way, today happened to be one of those days, so I sit in Liam's living room watching Genesis play with toys her dad has bought for her. Eventually, Genesis' cries convert to sniffles, and then she finally begins to calm down.

"Okay, I think Genesis might be all right," I say to Liam. "I should head out now."

"You should stay a while longer," he says, abruptly. "I want to spend some…" Liam thinks to himself for a moment as his thoughts trail off, and I'm not surprised when he doesn't pick up where he left off. I think Liam decided to go with a different choice of words and instead he says, "Genesis does look content, but it would be nice to have the company."

I don't know if I should stay any longer. I feel like it might not be the best idea to spend time with Liam. It's obvious he's been gradually trying to talk to me more, and I feel like some days, Liam is trying to rekindle a spark that will never reignite. A flame that permanently went out when he decided to abandon his family.

"You should stay and eat lunch with us," Liam insists.

I glance at him for a moment, unable to decipher his true intentions and turn my focus back to Genesis. "Oh, um. I don't know about that," I reply. I try to fabricate an excuse to leave. "I think I need to… uh, go and—"

"Please, stay for a little," Liam pleads. "I can whip something up real fast."

Liam whipping something up… in the kitchen? I have a difficult time imagining him cooking, let alone standing in the kitchen.

"Uh," I stutter and look at the clock on his wall as if I might have somewhere else to be… which I don't. "All right, maybe just a quick lunch," I say.

"Okay, great!" Liam says and rubs his hands together like he's some famous chef about to make us a five-star meal.

*****

One time, Liam tried to swoon me with a meal he prepared all by himself. It had to have been our fourth or fifth date—back when Liam still thought it was important to impress me. It was basically a culinary disaster.

We sat on a bench in front of the lily pond at Balboa Park as Liam pulled out a container from his backpack. My mouth began to water as I anticipated devouring our yummy lunch.

"I'm so excited, Liam. What did you make?" I asked, anxiously.

"Pasta salad," he replied.

"Ooo, I love pasta salad," I said while I popped open the lid. The first thing I noticed was it had olives. That was fine. I could work around them.

"What's the matter?" Liam asked.

I guess I gave myself more credit than I deserved. Liam could tell I wasn't super enthused about the meal he prepared.

"Uh, nothing," I responded as I continued to stare at the odd ingredients Liam had chosen.

"Hopefully you like it. No one's really taught me how to cook," he mentioned.

"Is that bologna you chopped up?"

"Yes—oh, sorry, you don't like bologna?" he asked.

"No, no… I do," I explained. "I've just never had it in pasta salad before." I've also never had cold cheesy pasta before, but I decided it was best not to mention that too. "But I guess there's a first time for everything," I chuckled, awkwardly.

"I wasn't quite sure how to make a cheese sauce, so I thought the liquid spray cheese was a good alternative," Liam added. "Maybe I should've gone a different route."

"No, it looks good," I lied.

My stomach churned when Liam told me about his thought process for using artificial cheese instead of the real deal. I tried hard to not look disgusted as I thought about eating Liam's strange pasta concoction. I tried to think positive. After all, he did throw some normal veggies in, like tomatoes and carrots. I've eaten worse things in my life… I think.

"I can buy us something else if this doesn't sound good to you," Liam suggested.

I shook my head. "I bet it's delicious," I told him.

I didn't want to be rude or offend Liam. I wanted our relationship to last longer than all my previous ones. So, I dug in and took a bite. I took one for the team.

"What do you think?" Liam asked, looking at me intently while waiting for my review.

Loud crunches escaped from my mouth as I chewed on pieces of rotini. "Mmm," I said and forced myself to take a big gulp. "Uh, the pasta's pretty al dente," I mentioned, and by "al dente" I meant it was straight up raw.

Liam slouched over, embarrassed. "Sorry, I guess I should've tasted it to see if it was done."

"No worries. It's... pretty good," I lied again. I readied myself to take another bite of the worst pasta salad I had ever had in my life.

"Eva, you don't have to lie," he said. "I actually don't want to eat that after the sounds you made while chewing." Liam chuckled. "I will buy us something else to eat."

I silently thanked God for pardoning me from having to suffer from ingesting more undercooked pasta. Then, I laughed along with Liam to show him I didn't mind eating his salad, but on the inside, I was feeling annoyed he didn't take the first bite. I hoped my stomach wasn't planning on getting angry with me for eating that sketchy canned cheese. I couldn't believe Liam didn't even taste the pasta to see if it was done! That's, like, the number one rule of cooking—sample your food! How else are you supposed to know if it tastes good?

"All good cooks know this," my mom said during another one of her cooking lessons. "You must always taste your food before serving it to others."

"But what if it has something in it I don't like?" I asked.

"You taste it anyway."

"Even if it has olives?" I said, looking up at my mom.

My mom smiled warmly. "Yes, even if it has olives."

"But why?" I asked, young and naive. "No mercy?"

My mom laughed at me and said, "You want people to enjoy your meal. What if it needs more soy sauce or oyster sauce?" She pointed to the chow fun sauce simmering on the stove. "No one likes a bland sauce on their noodles," my mom responded. "You want the people you are feeding to feel your food is worth eating."

The way my mom was talking, you'd have thought I was preparing a meal for the Queen of England. She grabbed a pair of chopsticks out of the drawer and handed one of the sticks to me.

After I dipped the end of a chopstick into the pot and tasted the sauce, my mom patted the top of my head. "How does it taste, Hunny?" my mom asked, and then she did the same and tested the sauce too.

"Hmm," I said as different flavors danced on my tongue. "I think… I think we should put a little more oyster sauce."

My mom looked pleased with my suggestion. "Good job, Hunny. I was thinking the exact same thing," she said.

This is when I learned *food is a form of validation.*

Genesis holds onto her musical bear as I pick her up off the floor. I'm happy I'm able to spend a while longer with her. "So, what are you planning on making," I ask Liam, sincerely curious.

He pulls out a large bowl and a bag of salad, and I

realize Liam's going to use a pre-made salad kit to make us lunch. I guess I am relieved because this *is* something edible and also quick. I'm pretty sure there's no chance anyone can mess up mixing a few ingredients together in a bowl. Also, Liam's salad choice doesn't look half-bad, but I'm not so sure how Genesis is going to feel about it.

I watch him pour the bacon bits, premade chicken, and croutons into the bowl with the lettuce. This must be the first time I've ever seen Liam hold salad spoons in his hands. I'm surprised Liam is even aware of such kitchen tools.

"Well, thanks for making lunch for us," I say, remembering to be thankful. "Do you feed Genesis salad often?"

Chloe, Liam's cat, rubs against my leg and purrs. I look down for a moment to admire her long gray fur and folded ears. Chloe seems to be enjoying our company just as much as Liam.

"Yes, sometimes. Genesis doesn't like the lettuce as you probably know, but she's a big fan of the chicken and bacon." Liam's smile is warm as he looks at me, and I feel like I'm looking at a completely different person.

How could this be the same person that treated me like a house servant? The same individual that took me for granted for multiple years. The guy who never lifted a finger to help with housework. If the twilight zone was a real thing, I'm in it, *for sure.*

The back of Liam's hand brushes his hair away from

his eyes. "I know it's nothing compared to the meals you've made me," he says.

"It looks like a really yummy salad," I assure him.

As Liam grabs a couple bowls, he points to my forearm. "You've been painting?" he asks. There's a small, dried patch of acrylic paint leftover on my skin.

"Oh, yeah, I must've missed that spot," I say as I try to rub the flakes off my arm.

"That's great, Eva. You were given a wonderful gift," Liam says.

Liam's compliment makes me feel a little uncomfortable. "I suppose," I reply.

Liam's compliments eventually dissipated after our first year or two as a couple. After the honeymoon stage was over, kind words were rare to come by—basically nonexistent.

"Is someone's birthday coming up?" he asks, knowing it was common for me to gift my paintings.

"No… I was actually planning on trying to sell a few of them. Maybe online or something."

"Oh, that's a great idea!" Liam says a little too enthusiastically.

I shrug. "Well, we will see. People might not want to buy them."

"I wouldn't worry about that," he says while smirking.

We sit down at the large dining table meant for more than just three people. "So, Eva, I want to talk to you about something," Liam says.

"Oh, yeah?" I say with my mouth full. "What about?"

Liam looks nervous, which isn't something that happens too often. "Uh… I want to talk about… me leaving you and Genesis," he says. Liam's voice has become quieter—more timid like he is ashamed of his mistake.

Oh gosh. Maybe I shouldn't have stayed, I think to myself. I swallow my crouton prematurely, and it scrapes the back of my throat. "Mm, oh, okay," I manage to say and quickly grab my glass of water.

Liam doesn't try to make eye contact with me. "I, um—I never apologized to you and Genesis, but I want you to know… I really am sorry for leaving." One of Liam's hands makes a fist, and he hammers it onto the edge of the table in slow motion. He finally looks up at me in sincerity and says, "I realized *I* ruined my life by giving up my family."

Wow, I thought I would never hear those words from Liam's mouth. My eyes widen, and I take another bite of my salad, using it as an excuse not to respond. I nod my head to show I understand and possibly forgive him, even though I'm pretty sure I'm still holding a solid grudge.

"It's kind of ironic." Liam chuckles uncomfortably to himself. "After I moved out of my parent's house and purchased my own place, I not only realized I was lonely, but I figured out that I completely messed things up with you. Since I've been thinking about how I ruined our relationship, I also began thinking about how I took you for granted. I wish I understood sooner how much you did for me when we were together."

I continue to sit silently, shoving my face with food as mixed feelings run rampant throughout my body. What Liam is saying seems so surreal. He *is* a completely different person.

Wait a minute! I think to myself—halting all positive thoughts about Liam. I decide to only let the negative ones filter through, so Liam doesn't suck me into his trap lined with candy-coated words. I won't let him fool me.

Yeah, Liam. I was not only your lover but also your personal cook and maid. Must suck to have to do all those things on your own now! How are you even capable of sifting Chloe's cat poop out of her litter box? Did you buy yourself one of those expensive automated scoopers that does it for you? I'm sure you did!

"You showed me how much you cared for me, and I didn't deserve you," he says. Liam is really showing off his persistence this afternoon. "If I could go back in time, I would make sure you knew you meant everything to me."

I feel my heart finally start to beat more freely, and my hate for Liam is slowly being released. The grudge I held onto so securely is fleeing from my grasp.

Liam continues apologizing and says, "I'm sorry for hurting you, Eva."

I pause from stuffing my face and smile at him. I take a deep breath and reply, "I forgive you, Liam. I'm happy you decided you want Genesis to be a part of your life." And, finally, I'm not lying.

Liam's eyes transport me back to our first date on the beach. There's lust written all over his gaze. "Your forgiveness means a lot to me," he says and reaches across the table to caress my hand. The way he is looking at me reminds me of the passion we once had.

I become lost in a distant thought and allow Liam to show physical affection toward me… for a minute too long. Once I force myself out of an old memory, I quickly retract my hand and place it on my lap.

"Uh, Liam… just because I forgive you, doesn't mean we will ever get back together."

Liam's calm demeanor quickly vanishes. "I've changed. Eva, I can be a good father and husband now," Liam says, becoming frustrated.

"Wait… Husband?" I ask, shocked. "Like you want to get married?"

"Yeah, I can make things right," he says, trying to persuade me.

"But you do know I'm still seeing Brian, right?" I mean, Liam *has to* know this.

"In all honesty, I was hoping you weren't seeing each other anymore," Liam says.

"Brian and I are still together," I say, sternly and cross my arms in front of my chest.

"Okay, but you don't love him. You and Brian—it's nothing like what we had." This was not a question at all, and Liam's voice is getting louder the longer our conversation goes on.

My emotions are screaming at the top of their lungs. I am not about to have a debate with Liam! Especially one about whether I love Brian or not.

"Uh, you know, maybe I should just go and let you spend some time with Genesis," I suggest, standing up from the table.

Liam breathes in deeply, holds the air in his lungs for a second, and says, "Please, Eva, I'm sorry." Calm returns to his face and his voice lowers. "I didn't mean to upset you. Let's just finish eating lunch."

Wow, two apologies in one day? From Liam? I'm *definitely* in the twilight zone.

I sigh and don't sit back down. "Liam, I really appreciate your apology and making me lunch today. I'm really happy you want Genesis back in your life. I know she will bring as much joy into your world as she does mine, but just to make things clear… Genesis is the only one coming back into your life. I don't mind a quick, five-minute exchange, four times a month, but I don't think we should be doing this whole lunch thing again or even—"

"Okay! I get it!" Liam shouts, interrupting my rant and walks toward the kitchen with his head down.

I kiss Genesis goodbye and she starts to pout, but

just slightly. Thank goodness the waterworks didn't start up again because I need to leave right this minute!

"I will see you tomorrow night when I pick up Genesis," I tell Liam.

He walks over to Genesis to clean off her tray but doesn't look at me. "Okay, see you then," he says, sadly.

I head to my car feeling like I just went through a high school breakup. It felt weird because we haven't been together the last two years. I suppose Liam has some closure now and can move on, or at least I hope so. I still cannot believe he made me lunch. I think Liam might still be in love with me. I mean, he did make me a salad!

Chapter Six

Liam Wong

I remove Genesis' tray and place it into the sink. I think about what I could've said to convince Eva to stay with me. What could I have said differently to make her want to be with me? She could've been mine forever. I wonder if Eva would've gotten back with me if it weren't for that arrogant, body-building boyfriend of hers. I really hate that guy.

As I set Genesis on the floor, I think about how my daughter is truly magnificent. I imagine Genesis entering the world for the first time while everyone admired her angelic beauty. She got her looks from her mother. Genesis' characteristics are more like Eva's than mine, which is probably a good thing. I remember Eva mentioning how she hoped our daughter would have my unique, amber-brown eyes and my odd, goofy ears. I'm not sure how attractive our daughter would've turned out if Eva's wishes had come true.

I regret missing out on the first year of Genesis' life, and lately, I've been finding myself reminiscing on past conversations I had with Eva. I don't know what I was thinking, giving up so much. A successful career didn't fill my house with love, and it didn't fill my stomach with delicious, home-cooked meals. I should have never let my mom convince me I had made a mistake investing myself in Eva.

"You are ruining your life!" my mom yelled, scolding me on the phone after her 51st birthday dinner. I left Eva crying in the living room just minutes ago before calling my mother.

"Mom, it will be fine. Trust me," I said, making sure to speak quietly so Eva wouldn't hear my phone call. "I'm almost done with my internship at the pharmacy, and then my income will be more than double what I'm currently making. I will easily be able to provide for the three of us."

There was no point in attempting to convince my mother. Once she had her mind made up, there was no changing it. Also, my mom's voice was stern. If God was a woman, God would have the exact same voice as hers.

"You should've been married before you decided to move in with Eva."

"I—"

"And remember what I told you when you first introduced us to her?"

"Yes, Mom. I remember."

"I told you that girl was going to be a bad influence on you."

"I know," I said, submissively.

"See, now look where it's gotten you. She has gotten you into a position you regret. Isn't that right?"

"Okay, Mom, I understand where you are coming from," I told her. It was useless to argue with God, so I didn't even try.

"You will be the subject of every conversation. All your aunties and uncles will talk about how you got Eva pregnant, and how you guys aren't even married. Not to mention, this is a terrible example for your younger brother!"

Many times, I've tried to hide my parents' opinion from Eva—mostly my mom's judgments. Although, she was careful enough to only talk badly about Eva when she wasn't present. Every time my mother and father mentioned Eva's job at the cafe being just a job and not a career—I would bring up the fact that she cooked and cleaned for me. I told them she took good care of me in an attempt to get them off my back, even though I never mentioned it to Eva. Everything Eva did for me I took for granted, and no matter what I told my parents, no matter what Eva did or didn't do, she was never good enough for their eldest son.

"So, now what are you going to do?" my mom asked, angrily. "You going to ask Eva to marry you, or do you want to be stuck with her and a baby out of wedlock?"

"I don't know. I need some time to decide," I told her. "Maybe the whole marriage thing."

"You can do better," she told me. "There's always another option. We can pretend like it never happened."

At the time, I believed my mother, and that's when I started to think about leaving Eva and my unborn baby. Eventually, I did just that. I left my pregnant girlfriend. I was such an asshole.

I think back to one of the most memorable dates I had with Eva. The time when we went to San Francisco for our one-year anniversary as boyfriend and girlfriend. That weekend was unforgettable.

Eva spent countless hours researching restaurants and places to see at the city by the bay. She planned out every aspect of our trip since I could never come up with any plans. Eva never made me feel guilty for lame Valentine's Days or having to urge me to get out of the house for a date night. Eva probably thought I didn't care enough to ever surprise her, but that was never the case. I was just terrible at coming up with ideas—never great at the romance thing.

I recall having dinner with Eva at this two-story

restaurant, which reminded me of a large 80s diner but a bit more modern. It was right on Fisherman's Wharf. I had the most amazing crab of my life that night, and I will never forget Eva's face when she took the first bite out of her dessert. The powdered sugar from the beignets covered her entire mouth.

"Oh, my gosh! These are so good! Like, amazing-good!" Eva managed to say with her mouth full. She finished off the fried donut in two bites, which was extremely rare for her. Eva was always such a slow eater. "It's like I'm eating clouds… from Heaven!" she said. I was amused because my date looked like an adorable chipmunk with her cheeks jam-packed. She ignored my laughter and continued to inhale the fried dough. I even recall Eva choking on the powdered sugar for a split-second, but it hardly hindered her eating frenzy. Watching Eva fall in love with the food in San Francisco made the trip worthwhile and one I will never forget. I wish we could go back to those days.

I look at Genesis' hearing aid and it saddens me. I know Eva told me Genesis has been developing at a normal rate for a one-year-old, but I can't help but worry a little about her future. I know I should be more knowledgeable about her hearing loss, but I don't because I wasn't there to learn about it alongside Eva. It's hard for me to answer simple questions from strangers when I take Genesis shopping with me. Even when we see friends and family, it's hard for me to explain all the details and needs of Genesis' hearing loss. No one is more disappointed in me than I am.

I should have treated Eva with more respect and loved her like I could lose her, but instead, I treated her like I would be able to keep her around forever as long as *I* saw fit. My life would be completely different if I hadn't screwed up everything. I could have a family, but I don't. We could be happily celebrating every holiday together, but I don't see that in our future. I should be the one tucking Genesis into bed and keeping Eva warm at night, but I'm not. My family is broken… because of me.

"Hey, Genesis, Daddy got you a new toy," I say. "You want to see it?" I join her on the floor and hand her a toy phone. "Your mommy told me these are your favorite."

Genesis excitedly yanks it out of my hand. The buttons light up and make sounds as she pushes them. She holds the phone to her ear, smiles, and looks up at me. "Da-da!" Genesis says, happily.

This is the first time Genesis has acknowledged me as her father. The very first time.

I hug her, and my eyes begin to fill with tears. "I love you, Genesis," I tell her. "I'm not giving up on us being a family. I promise you… we will be a family again."

Whatever it takes.

Chapter Seven

The Dress

You look absolutely stunning!" Brandi's mom says, clasping her hands together below her chin. There's a glimmer in her eye as she looks at her beautiful daughter walk out of the dressing room.

"Thank you. I was hoping that's what you were going to say," Brandi replies, semi-jokingly and hugs Julie.

"Although, it is very form-fitting for a wedding dress," Julie adds.

Julie is Brandi's mom. The first time I saw Julie pick up Brandi from school, I thought she was Brandi's older sister. Julie had Brandi when she was only seventeen and out of wedlock. But unlike Liam's and my story, Mrs. Ryan had her happy ending with Brandi's dad.

"That's how it's supposed to be!" Brandi says and

shakes her head back and forth at her mom's comment.

"You are quite a sight," Brandi's grandma chimes in. "But, you know, I bet you could've turned my old wedding dress into something just as nice, and for half the price!"

This is the first time Brandi's family and I have seen her in her elegant wedding dress, and now I'm starting to see why Brandi went dress shopping by herself. I was so sad when Brandi told me she wanted to pick out her dress alone.

"What bride does that?" I asked Brandi.

"Uh, one that doesn't want to deal with her mom's or grandma's harsh opinions," she replied. "The last thing I need is for them to try to dictate which dress I should buy."

"Well, I can come with you. I will zip my lips so tight!" I promised my bestie. "And you know your mom and grandma would end up loving whichever dress you pick out anyway."

"You could, but if my family found out I excluded them and let you come, they would slaughter me like a pig," Brandi explained. "And you don't know what they are like. You weren't there when my mom took me to find my dress for winter formal during our sophomore year. She kept bringing me the most hideous dresses to try on, and the ones I liked… let's just say, she definitely had something to say about every one of them."

I sighed. "Ugh, fine! I guess I can wait," I said, disappointed.

I tried to be understanding.

Brandi's mermaid dress hugs her perfect body, and she looks flawless. The lace is vintage but also all the rage. She told me she had to get her dress taken in at the hips. I wasn't all that surprised since she has a body like a model, and because of the alterations, the dress looks like it was made specifically for her. I wasn't sure how anyone could find anything negative to say.

"You look amazing, Brandi," I say. "Your dress is perfect."

A wide grin consumes Brandi's face, and she does her normal excited pee-pee dance with her legs. "I know!" she shouts and hugs me.

Brandi gives me a head-to-toe look-over. "You look amazing in your dress too!" Brandi says. "I couldn't have picked out a better—"

"Eva, you look like a floozy!" Brandi's grandma shouts. I look at Grandma Rose and then at my reflection in the long freestanding mirror outside of the dressing rooms.

"Grandma Rose!" Brandi yells. "She does not!"

I've only met Grandma Rose one other time, and I learned she was just as blunt as my dad.

I held out my hand, introducing myself to Brandi's

grandma after our graduation ceremony.

"It's so nice to finally meet you, Ms. Rose," I said.

She didn't shake my hand. "I don't like being called Ms. Rose," she told me, sharply. "Makes me feel old."

Brandi cringed, knowing how her grandma tended to act. "I tried to warn you," Brandi whispered into my ear.

I kept my focus on Grandma Rose. "Oh, I'm sorry. I—"

"You looked petrified on that stage, Sweetie." Grandma Rose told me. "Like a deer in headlights."

The fact that she called me Sweetie didn't make her words any kinder, and it left me speechless. Even with Brandi's warning, I would have never guessed Grandma Rose would have been so open with her feelings. Her smile was warm and her body fragile with age, which was very misleading.

I shrug at my reflection. Then, I stare at my hot pink tube top dress that sits just below my butt cheeks and tilt my head to look at my dress from a different angle, but the dress looks even more revealing. "Well, she's not wrong," I tell Brandi.

"Oh, whatever, Eva!" Brandi says, annoyed. "You and Michelle both look ridiculously amazing in your dresses! Doesn't matter what anyone else says!"

Brandi scavenges for her phone in her purse and shows me the picture of her soon-to-be sister-in-law, Michelle. Michelle had sent Brandi a model-esk picture of her in her bridesmaid dress.

When I looked at the picture, I thought of how Michelle looked nothing like her brother, Max. Michelle was thin and tall like Brandi but with beautiful wavy red-orange hair that reminded me of an endless sunset. The combination of Grandma Rose telling me I look like a hooch and the picture of Max's sister made me feel a little insecure.

"Your boobs look good, girl," Brandi tells me, noticing my apprehensiveness.

"You always say that," I say, laughing. "And for the record… I don't believe you."

"You girls want to go get some lunch?" Mrs. Ryan asks. "Grandma Rose says she will treat you ladies."

"Ooo, sushi?" Brandi asks, hopeful.

"Oh, whatever Bridezilla wants," Grandma Rose says and chuckles to herself. I couldn't tell if Brandi's grandma was serious or joking, but then I realize where Brandi gets her feistiness from.

"I will have the sashimi and nigiri combo," I tell the server.

"You got it!" he tells me and goes to put our orders in.

"So, Eva, Brian told me you two have been dating the last few months," Mrs. Ryan says. "Seems like he's becoming really attached to you and Genesis. I've also heard you girls have been staying over at my son's condo too."

"Oh, uh, yeah," I say, not really knowing how to carry on the conversation.

I think Julie seems happy for us, but at the moment I was thinking of how Liam's mom reacted when Liam told her we were moving in together. I quickly remind myself Mrs. Ryan isn't like that. I don't think Mrs. Ryan cares if Genesis and I spend the night at her son's place even though we aren't married.

"What was that you said?" Grandma Rose says, curiously. "I thought my grandson was still with that darling girl, Clarissa."

Brandi quietly slams her palm onto the table. "Grandma! I told you Brian dumped her a while ago," Brandi says and looks at me sympathetically. "You know how she forgets," she reminds me.

"It's okay. I know," I say. I bite my lip and try to think of how to respond to Grandma Rose's comment. "Uh, I—"

The server sets down our miso soups and salads, which gives me a moment to think of something to say. "Thank you," I say, looking up at our waiter, more grateful for his interruption rather than the food.

I look at Grandma Rose and Mrs. Ryan sitting across from us, who are impatiently waiting for my response. I regain my composure and tell them, "Yeah, Brian and I have been seeing each other for about six months now. He's really great with Genesis, and she's become really fond of him."

"That's lovely, Sweetie," Grandma Rose responds and then takes a sip of her soup.

"How come you and Brian haven't brought Genesis over lately?" Brandi's mom asks. "I haven't seen her in a lifetime."

"Oh, yeah. I guess it has been a little while," I reply.

"The last time I think I saw her was at her 1st birthday party," Mrs. Ryan says. "You girls need to come and spend some time with us. Genesis has another set of grandparents that want to see her, you know."

That is so nice of Mrs. Ryan to say. I smile at her, nod my head, and reply, "Okay, we will make it a priority to spend some time with you. I will tell my parents they have to share. They do see her pretty often." In fact, I'm confident my parents were thoroughly enjoying their time with their sweet granddaughter this afternoon.

I take a bite of my salmon sashimi and it melts in my mouth. "Mmm, thank you, Grandma Rose. This lunch is really great," I mention, in hopes of making a good impression on her. I hope she thinks I'm as "darling" as Clarissa.

"Yeah, thank you, Grandma Rose," Brandi adds.

Brandi's grandma doesn't acknowledge our gratitude. Instead, she asks me, "So, are you and Brian going to have a baby anytime soon?"

A piece of fish becomes lodged in my throat as a result of Grandma Rose's nosey question. I place my hand across my chest and look at Brandi. Brandi's elbow is on the table, and her hand is placed on top of her forehead. She's looking down at her California roll and slowly shaking her head. Grandma Rose has no filter.

"Oh, dear. Are you choking, Sweetie?" Grandma Rose asks.

I pat my chest—encouraging the food to cooperate, but I continue to choke. Brandi looks at me urgently. "Stand up, Eva," Brandi instructs, calmly. "I can give you the Heimlich."

I wave my hand in the air and swallow deeply, but it doesn't help my situation. I try to throw my back toward the back of the booth, which also doesn't work.

"Dammit! Eva. Stand up!" Brandi shouts, pushing me out of the booth. "Your face is turning blue." I look at Grandma Rose and Julie as Brandi wraps her arms around my abdomen. They both look horrified, which makes me panic and place my hands over my throat. "Don't worry. I got you," Brandi reassures me and thrusts her closed fists into my stomach.

Out of the corner of my eye, I see an old pervy man wink at me as he witnesses Brandi shove her body into the back of mine for a second time.

"Third time is a charm!" Brandi yells. I gasp for air as soon as the piece of fish dislodges from my throat. Everyone watches the chunk of fish fly through the air in slow motion and slap Grandma Rose on her forehead.

I cringe. "Oopsie…" I say.

It doesn't seem to faze her. Grandma Rose grumbles and says, "I've had worse things teabag my forehead." She continues enjoying her lunch like nothing happened.

Brandi and I look at each other in complete and utter shock. How does Grandma Rose even know that term? Maybe she meant it differently… or maybe she didn't.

Brandi and I slide back into the booth and Grandma Rose begins where she left off. "You know I want at least four more great-grandchildren before I croak. I assumed Brian would've had some with Clarissa years ago," she tells me, or more like the entire table. "That didn't seem to work out, and now my grandson has to start all over again—from scratch." Grandma Rose shakes her head. "That's too bad. I really wanted those grandbabies by now."

"Grandma!" Brandi screams again.

"Yeah… Well, we haven't talked too much about it, Grandma Rose," I explain. "I think we should probably get married first. Don't you think?"

But again, I remember that doesn't matter to Brandi's family. Julie did seem pretty happy when I confirmed how far my relationship with her son had progressed, and Grandma Rose is really set on having those grandbabies. I doubt my parents would be too happy if I were to have another baby out of wedlock. Actually, I know for a fact they would be upset.

"Hmph," Brandi's Grandma says, and goes back to eating her lunch. She's obviously disappointed in my answer.

Once we finish our lunch, Grandma Rose takes her credit card out of the sleeve and puts it back into her purse. She hands Brandi the bill and asks, “Can you write down the tip for me, Sweetie?”

“Of course, Grandma.”

“Your mother says I never tip enough,” Grandma Rose explains.

“Well, it’s true,” Julie says, defending herself. “You are supposed to tip at least fifteen percent and twenty if the service was good. Everyone knows this.”

“Okay, Julie!” Grandma Rose says to her daughter and then points at Brandi. “Give the server twenty percent. I enjoyed looking at his tight ass.”

“Oh gosh, Grandma,” Brandi says, and we all start to laugh, except for Grandma Rose… because she is *dead* serious!

Chapter Eight

Surprise Lunch Date

I struggle to find the key to Brian's condo. I fumble through multiple sets of keys while holding onto bags of groceries and balancing Genesis on my hip. Once I manage to let myself inside, I set down the groceries on Brian's kitchen counter and turn on the TV for Genesis. I quickly turn the volume down because the last thing I want is to wake up Brian. Brian always tells me how he never sleeps well when he has to work graveyards.

I decided to start our weekend off with a nice lunch together and surprise Brian with one of his favorite dishes. I heat up a pan of oil for the wonton strips. Then, I pull out the roasted chicken from the bag and begin to shred the meat into a bowl. I haven't made Brian Chinese chicken salad for a couple months, and I know he's been craving it. I think he enjoys the dressing the most. He's told me that my family's recipe rivals even the best restaurant dressings.

I finish frying up the wontons and set a few of the cooled ones in a bowl for Genesis to snack on while she watches her favorite show. Genesis loves crunchy foods, and I happily watch her mac down a fistful of wonton strips.

I'm just about to pour the lettuce into a large bowl when the doorbell rings. I didn't think Brian was expecting anyone this afternoon. I wipe my hands on the towel hanging on the stove handle and make my way over to the front door.

There's a woman with ginger-red hair standing outside of Brian's condo.

"Clarissa?" I say, surprised.

Clarissa looked exactly the same as she did in high school. Her hair is still tied back tightly in a mid-pony just like I remembered from our teenage days—the one and only hairstyle I've ever seen on her. Clarissa's face is still sprinkled generously with freckles. I remember telling Brandi that Clarissa reminded me of a cute Lindsay Lohan. The only small difference in Clarissa's appearance, between high school and now, are the small crow's feet around her eyes. They were most prominent when she forced a smile on her face and said, "Um, hi, Eve… It's Eve, right?"

I couldn't tell if Clarissa was being passive-aggressive and pretending not to know my name. I tried not to linger on that thought too long.

"Close, it's actually Eva. But anyway… how are you doing?" I ask, pulling the door shut so all Clarissa can see is me standing in the doorway. This was me, *not* inviting her in.

Clarissa glares at me. "So, what are you doing here? Is Brandi here too?"

"No, she's not," I reply. "Brian and I have been seeing each—"

Clarissa cuts me off. "Oh, I see. I'm surprised Brian didn't mention anything about you."

Now I'm positive Clarissa is the most passive-aggressive person I've ever come in contact with. I wonder if she only acts this way towards women. I have a hard time believing Brian would want to be with someone with that type of character flaw.

"Anyway, I haven't been too bad. I was just here to drop off the rest of Brian's things he left at our apartment," Clarissa explains, and now I notice she is holding a small box that can't have more than three or four things in it.

"Oh, okay. I can go ahead and give those to Brian when he wakes up," I say reaching for the box, but Clarissa abruptly pulls it in closer to her body like she is protecting it from my prying hands.

"Sorry, um, I was actually hoping *I* could give Brian

his belongings," she says. Clarissa looked peeved at my presence. I know I was *definitely* irritated at hers!

I hear Brian come out of his bedroom and see him quickly pull his shirt over his head. He looks flustered. "Hey, Eva, I didn't know you were going to be over so early today," he tells me and gives me a kiss on my forehead. "Uh, hey Clarissa," he says. She smiles at him, and I try not to give his *darling* ex-girlfriend an evil stare. "Thanks for bringing my stuff back," Brian tells her.

I remove my hand from the side of the door due to Brian forcing it open wider. Clarissa looks at me briefly like she wishes I would disappear, and then she speaks to Brian. "Do you think we can talk for a minute?"

"Yeah, of course. What's going on?" Brian asks as all three of us continue to stand at the front door.

Clarissa keeps looking at me while she talks to Brian, and I'm beginning to take offense to her glances. "Like… in private?" she asks.

"Yeah—uh, sure," Brian responds. "I'll be right back," he tells me and walks out of the condo. I try not to panic as Brian shuts the door behind him.

"What the—" I say to myself.

I contemplate about pushing my ear against the door and attempt to listen in on their conversation but decide against it. Instead, I finish making the dressing and toss the salad. By the time lunch is complete, five minutes has already passed. I sit Genesis at the table with me and we begin eating our lunch without Brian.

I'm still trying not to worry. "I guess it's just the two of us, little lady," I tell Genesis and place some chicken in front of her. "It's fine… It will be fine," I say, unsuccessfully reassuring myself. My daughter is too busy stuffing her face to notice I'm talking.

I attempt to tranquilly plan out what I want to ask Brian when he is done talking to Clarissa. Obviously, I want answers, and his answers better be good! Like… he better put on his mind-reading cap before I completely lose my shit. All right, maybe that's not the calmest conversation I've ever planned out, but who can blame me? I'm completely freaking out, to say the least.

"Sorry about that, Eva," Brian says, sitting down to join us for lunch. My bowl is almost empty. Brian still looks flustered, and I know for a fact my face is projecting all my emotions, especially the crazy, irrational ones.

"You didn't mention you were talking to Clarissa again," I say, calmly.

"Oh, yeah… I guess I didn't. Well, she only texted me a couple of days ago asking if it would be all right if she dropped off a few of my things I left at our old place," Brian explains. "I didn't think you were going to be over this early, or I would've told her to come by at a different time."

I don't know how I feel about his answer. Would he have invited Clarissa in if I wasn't at his condo? Would he have talked to her longer and reminisced about the past? Would they have watched a movie together? More specifically, would they have watched a *Disney* movie? My heart pounds at the thought of me "ruining" their time with one another.

"So, what did Clarissa want to talk about?" I ask, still trying to stay cool.

"Uh, she just wanted to know how I was doing and whatnot."

Such a vague answer. "What did you tell her?"

"Not much, just that I've been good."

Another useless answer! "Hmm… Okay, so are you planning on keeping in touch with her?"

"I wasn't… really planning on it," Brian says, uncomfortably.

I stare Brian down. "Are you? Yes or no?" I'm sick of Brian dancing around the subject.

He pokes his fork in his salad a few times—stalling, which makes my blood heat up. "Clearly, you are upset," he says.

I purse my lips. "Mhmm."

"I don't want Clarissa to get in the middle of our relationship… So, I won't talk to her if that's what you want."

Uh, yeah! That is *exactly* what I want. Seriously, Brian, if this was the other way around… wait. Now I feel a bit hypocritical thinking about the lunch I had with Liam, which leads me to think Clarissa might be trying to weasel her way back into Brian's life!

I try to dig a little deeper. "So, what stuff did she need to drop off anyway?"

"Uh, just a couple of toiletries and one of my shirts she found in her closet," he replies. Obviously, nothing he was in dire need of… ever.

"Hmm, all right," I say, skeptical. "Is Clarissa dating anyone right now?" I ask. I don't think Brian is aware of what I'm trying to uncover with my "sneaky-girl" questions.

"I'm not really sure. I don't think she is. Why?"

"Just curious," I lie. I breathe in deeply, hoping Brian has a good answer for my next question that has been put on the back burner for some time. "So, I know you've told me Clarissa wanted different things in life and that's why you left her, but what *actually* happened between the two of you? I know there has to be more to the story."

Brian starts to poke at his food again before answering me. "I, um—" he murmurs.

He finally looks up at me and sets his forearm on the table like he's about to tell me some bad news—kind of what I would imagine if he were to tell me a family member passed away or something.

"Before I moved into my condo and was living with Clarissa, I thought she was the one I was going to spend the rest of my life with."

Oh, my gosh. This *is* bad news.

Brian's words are like a needle filled with

Novocain—stabbed directly into my beating heart, but he continues to explain, "I wanted to marry her, but every time I brought up marriage, Clarissa would tell me how she wasn't sure she wanted to be tied down, which was stupid. Sometimes, she would say that married couples get comfortable and take each other for granted. Other times, Clarissa would make excuses and tell me she needed to pay off some of her credit cards. Another time, she told me she wanted to travel first before tying the knot. Clarissa was full of bullshit. We were together for more than ten years, but she couldn't fully commit. At least, not in the way that I wanted."

I feel my throat start to tighten, and my eyes become watery. Brian quickly pulls his chair around the table to sit next to me and holds my hand with both of his.

"Please don't be upset, Eva," he tells me. "If I still thought Clarissa was the one, I wouldn't have asked you and Genesis to move in with me."

I start to relax a bit since there is some logic to what Brian is telling me, and I try not to think irrationally, but I can't help but wonder if Brian has already judged me for my inability to commit. I wonder if he thinks I'm incapable of a lasting future because I haven't agreed to live with him by now. If this is the case, maybe Brian's right. Maybe I'm having a hard time committing like Clarissa, but in my defense, I have my many reasons—Liam, Liam… and Liam.

I continue with my questions about his ex and ask,

"So, you said Clarissa just texted you a couple days ago asking to drop off your stuff?"

"Yeah," he replies, still holding my hand in his. "I really thought I grabbed everything when I moved out."

"I just find it kind of strange that Clarissa has been ignoring you for… forever, and all of a sudden, she drops off a couple nonessential items," I state.

"Well, uh… I've been meaning to tell you," Brian explains.

Oh, no. What now?

"Clarissa started texting me about a month ago."

Now my blood is like molten lava, and I try my best to suppress my fury. "What?" I stare blankly at Brian. "Seriously?"

"But—but this is the first time I've seen her since the breakup."

I pull my hand away from Brian's grasp. I cannot believe he just said a month. I need confirmation. "You've been talking to her for a… *month*? An entire month?"

"I wanted to tell you, but I also didn't want to upset you," Brian says and attempts to reach for my hand again, but I reject him.

"That's… *really* not okay that you kept that from me!" I yell, sadly. My temporary anger has transformed back into hurt.

"I'm sorry, Eva," he says, softly. "I won't keep talking to Clarissa. She just had some family problems recently and has been going through a rough time. Clarissa doesn't have that many people to talk to about her personal problems."

I'm so over hearing Brian explain why it's okay for him and Clarissa to talk to one another. I'm sick of hearing Brian speak his ex's name. I'm done with this subject, and I desperately want this argument to end. I want things to go back to how they were before Clarissa showed up at the condo!

"All right, well… as long as you make a clean cut with Clarissa, I will be fine." I try to produce a sincere smile on my face, but it still feels artificial.

"I love you, Eva," Brian says, and I allow him to caress my hand again. "I don't want you to be upset at me. Where else will I be able to get this amazing salad?"

Brian finally gets a genuine smile to produce itself on my face, and I can't help but giggle at his sweet words.

Chapter Nine

Awkward Appointment

"Hi, appointment for Genesis at 4:00?" Carol asks.

"Yeah, just to get an impression for another mold," I tell the receptionist.

"Oh, yes. Did you receive my message that Dr. Kearny had to leave early due to a family emergency?"

"No, sorry. I've been at work all day. I rushed over here," I explain. "I haven't looked at my phone since early this morning."

"That's not a problem, Miss Gin. I was just trying to get a hold of you to let you know of Dr. Kearny's absence, but Dr. Grayson was able to squeeze you in between his other appointments."

My heart transforms into a bolder and smashes into the bottom of my stomach. Oh, shit.

"Will that work out okay for you and Genesis?" Carol asks.

"Uh, yeah... that should be fine," I lie.

"Okay, Dr. Grayson should be out any minute."

I managed to avoid Ken for the last seven months or so, but I guess my streak has come to an end. Maybe this is a good thing, and we can have some more closure. I pray this appointment goes smoothly and try to stay positive.

"Hello, Eva, it's been a little while," Ken says.

I stand up with Genesis in my arms. "Hey... Yeah, it has been a while," I reply, awkwardly.

I felt more comfortable standing in front of Ken the time I had my breastmilk mishap and was wearing my saturated shirt along with my poop-stained pants. Yeah, this encounter is a hundred times worse. Why did Dr. Kearny have to have an emergency *today*?

"Right this way," Ken says as he leads me into the other room. "So, how has Genesis been?"

"Good. Her earmold is whistling pretty bad already," I tell him.

"Ah, no worries. We will go ahead and take an impression and get that taken care of." He grins. I had forgotten about Ken's prince-like smile, which is even more perfect than I remember.

I'm a little surprised Ken is handling himself so well. He is keeping things really professional.

"So, are you still seeing Brian?" he asks, looking down at the pink putty he is mixing with a small metal spatula.

Well, that was short-lived. "Uh, yeah. We are still together," I reply, hesitantly. I try to remove the focus away from myself. "How are you doing? Has your sister come down to visit you lately?"

Ken smirks, but I'm not quite sure why. "I've been doing really well, actually. I've been going to the beach almost every day to get my run in," Ken says and places the putty into a thick syringe. "I've been giving online dating a shot and have met a couple of nice girls."

So, now I understand the reason for his smirk. During his encounter with Brian at Genesis' birthday party, I had learned that Ken loses his modesty when he is upset. Also, I guess my question about his sister wasn't important enough for him to acknowledge.

"Oh, that's good," I say, hoping time moves a little quicker. Genesis keeps trying to pull out the string that is attached to the plug in her left ear, and I continue to keep her hand away.

"Yes, although, none of them have cooked me anything as appealing as you did on our first date," he mentions. Now Dr. Ken's face is inches away from mine as he slowly squeezes the putty into Genesis' ear. "What I would give to have your cooking one last time, Eva." Ken's dreamy blue eyes connect with mine before he takes a step back, which confirms he's still hung up on me.

I ignore Ken's comments about my cooking. "Uh, so, it should only take a couple weeks to get the new mold, right?" I ask, even though I already know the answer.

I am desperate to lessen the awkward moments, and I still sit impatiently with Genesis in my lap as she continues to fight for control of her arm.

"Here, Genesis," Dr. Grayson says, handing her a wooden maraca to keep her preoccupied. "Brian's really lucky to have a girl like you."

I can't tell if Ken's talking to me or Genesis. I just nod my head and smile.

"Let me see if it's dry," Ken says and touches his finger to the putty in my daughter's ear. "Nope, not yet. One more minute."

Dammit, another minute too long! He tries to converse with me again. "So, Eva. How are your parents doing?"

I can't help but think he's trying to remind me of how much my parents adored him. I think the not-so-modest side of Ken has *officially* overstayed its welcome.

"They are both doing really great. Thanks for asking," I say, attempting to be polite.

"I kind of miss chatting with your dad," he says.

If I could get down on my knees and pray for this appointment to be over, I would. "I'm sure he misses your conversations too," I say.

Finally, Ken pulls the dried putty out of Genesis' ear,

and I am one step closer to running out the door. "Let's go ahead and schedule an appointment with Carol to pick up Genesis' mold two weeks from now."

"All right," I say as Ken places his hand on my back and leads me to Carol's desk. I walk a little faster to avoid his touch.

"Well, it was such a pleasure seeing you, Eva," he says before heading back to the room. "If you need anything, feel free to call me, and when I say anything, I mean… anything at all."

Carol looks up from her computer and asks, "So, did you still want me to continue scheduling Genesis with Dr. Kearny or did you want to see Dr. Gray—"

"YES!" I shout. Then, I clear my throat and speak more calmly. "Yes… please. Dr. Kearny would be great."

Chapter Ten

Abandoned

While Genesis takes her afternoon nap, I decide to make some fried rice for Brian so he can have some throughout his work week coming up. Brian positions himself behind me and wraps his arms around my waist.

He whispers into my ear and says, "I'm going to take a shower. Do you want to join me?"

"I just started making you fried rice!" I reply, giggling.

"You can finish cooking after we shower," he suggests and places his lips on my bare skin. Brian has learned where the best places to kiss me are. One of many vulnerable spots on my body happens to be on the side of my neck.

"Okay, okay," I say and playfully shrug him off. "Let

me at least finish rinsing the rice out and get it into the cooker."

Brian undresses in front of me and my eyes stare at his perfectly toned body. I almost decide to leave the unwashed rice in the sink and join him for more than just a shower.

Brian continues to try to tempt me and begins doing strange motions with his hips—uncoordinated dance moves that include offbeat sways. Brian places his hands behind his head like people do when they are lying down and relaxing on the beach.

"What are you doing? Are you trying to dance?" I ask, entertained. Brian's unskillful dance moves are hilarious.

"Oh, come on! You know you like it!" he shouts.

I think I'm witnessing a sad audition for Thunder from Down Under. "Yeahhh… Hard pass," I say.

Brian ignores my comments that mock him. He obnoxiously swings his underwear above his head and throws them toward the bedroom. "Don't keep me waiting too long," he says, in the most ridiculously lame seductive voice I have ever heard.

I continue with my cooking as Brian turns on the shower. Then, I hear Brian's phone ring. "Hey! Someone's calling you!" I yell from the kitchen, but Brian can't hear me through the sounds of water pouring down, and he has missed the call.

I finish rinsing out the rice and start the cooker.

Brian's phone begins ringing again, and I begin to wonder if it's his work or an emergency. I decide it's best to answer the call just in case, so I quickly run over to Brian's phone.

"Hello?"

"Hi, um… Oh, Eve? Hey, it's Clarissa."

What the hell?

"Heyyy… Clarissa. Yeah, this is Eva. Eva… with an A… at the end. What's going on?" I say, extremely shocked.

I'm pretty sure Brian told me he wasn't going to talk to Clarissa anymore, and by pretty sure, I mean he most *definitely* was not supposed to keep in contact with her. There's no possible way there was any misunderstanding between Brian and me. I made my feelings pretty clear when Clarissa stopped by.

"Is Brian free to talk for a minute?" she asks, politely.

"Uh, he's actually in the shower... right now," I tell her.

"I see. Well, you can just let him know I'm sorry for not returning his call yesterday." She continues, "Tell him I'm off work today, and I will make sure I have my phone on me. Tell Brian if I don't hear from him, I will try back later tonight."

I want to tell Clarissa off so badly. I think about mentioning how it's inappropriate she's talking to my boyfriend. I should tell Clarissa she needs to back off like a crazed woman would do. I could straight-up tell Clarissa she had her chance and needs to find someone else. I want to scream into the phone and tell her Brian is mine now. I'm about to lash out at Clarissa and say a hundred hurtful things to her… but I bite my tongue instead.

"Sure, I will let him know," I say through my teeth.

"Oh, also, it was so funny, Eve. I had this vivid dream last night about Brian. He was at our apartment, and he was telling me how much he wanted to—"

"Sorry!" I shout. I don't want to find out what happens at the end of Clarissa's dream, so I decide to make up whatever excuse off the top of my head as quickly as possible. "Genesis just dropped a load in her diaper, so I have to go. Okay, bye!"

What is going on? What's happening between Brian and Clarissa? Why did Brian call Clarissa yesterday? How could he lie to me? I quickly decide to abandon making fried rice for Brian and begin gathering my things around the condo.

"Eva!" Brian yells from the shower. "Are you coming or what?"

I ignore him. My eyes begin to blur, filling with tears. I hear Brian turn off the water, and I try to disperse the moisture on my face with the back of my hand before he notices I've been crying.

"What's going on?" Brian asks, wrapping his towel around his waist. "What's the matter?" Brian tries to get a better look at my splotchy face and reaches out his hand to place it on the small of my back. "Why are you upset?"

Brian won't stop trying to console me and keeps coming nearer, but I continue to maneuver myself around him. I shake my head and hold out my arm, trying to keep him at a distance. "Come on. Please, tell me what's wrong," Brian says. "You're worrying me, Eva."

I am unable to manage my tears from falling onto my cheeks again. I look at him through my saddened eyes. "You told me you were going to stop talking to Clarissa!" I yell, and my angered words reverberate throughout the room.

"Oh, no. This isn't what you think it is. Please, don't do this, Eva," he says throwing his hands by his sides. "Let me explain. I can explain."

Brian tries to bring me in close to him again, but I refuse, pushing him away. "You said you wouldn't talk to her! You lied to me!" I scream. My hand claws at my chest, wishing the tightness around my heart would loosen. "Clarissa obviously wants to get back together with you! How do you not see that?"

"I don't think that's it, Eva. I think she just needs someone to talk to." Brian's voice is panicked as he tries to reason with me.

"Well, why does that person have to be you? Obviously, you have chosen Clarissa over Genesis and me! What you are doing with Clarissa is called emotional cheating!" I shout, fiercely. "Look it up!" Hurt and anger cloud my mind, and I continue to scream, "And that dumb bi—"

I stop myself from stooping down to Clarissa's level, but my enraged rant still goes on. "On top of everything else, your ex keeps calling me Eve! And on purpose!" I yell and hurriedly search for my keys through my blurred vision. I forcefully yank off the key to Brian's condo and dramatically throw my Valentine's Day gift onto the floor.

Brian has his hands out in front of him like a beggar who hasn't had a meal in days. "Please, Eva," Brian pleads. "Don't do this. Just give me a minute to explain."

I ignore him, scoop Genesis from her crib, and run out of the condo to escape Brian's betrayal. Genesis expresses her frustration toward me. She is one irritated girl, and I struggle to put her into the car seat.

Tears are staining my face, but I wipe my daughter's cheeks instead. I am screaming on the inside, but I soothe my baby girl and tell her everything will be all right. My heart is shattered, but I tend to my daughter's wants and needs.

I sit in the driver's seat and take a couple minutes to calm myself before driving to Brandi's. I glance out the window and see Brian half-naked in his cargo shorts and no shirt. He sprints down the stairs to try to stop me from leaving, but I pull away just before he gets to my car.

I abandon Mr. Right.

Chapter Eleven

Reality

I can feel Brian's chest contracting on top of mine. He breathes heavily on my neck and grips the side of my thigh—digging his hands into my skin. My fingertips slowly trace a line on his back, and I hear Brian's voice as he whispers into my ear and says, "Eva, you are so beautiful."

Both my hands clench the silky sheet I'm lying on, and my back arches. I'm unable to respond to Brian's lustful words because I'm too far gone. "I love you more than anything," Brian says. "I want to spend the rest of my life with you."

I slip even further with each word that leaves his lips.

My eyes shoot open, and I dab at the tears on my face that have collected from my dream. I glance at the sunshine beaming through the window—unsure if I have been awakened prematurely due to the sunrays or my crying daughter. Funny how dreams and nightmares can feel so real. I try to decide if I'm more disappointed that my dream wasn't reality or because it came to an end.

I roll myself off the couch bed and attend to Genesis. I pick her up out of her crib and hold my daughter close to my chest. I've felt like a real-life zombie since running out on Brian. I probably looked like one of the undead too. It hurts to yearn for someone you love, to say the least.

To ease my pain, I lean my head on top of Genesis' and try to erase my recent dream from my memories. I turn on one of Genesis' favorite movies, hoping she will let me snuggle her for a while longer. Whenever I'm down in the dumps, I can always find comfort in holding my baby girl.

Genesis grabs my phone off the armrest. "No, no, Genesis. This is Mommy's," I say. I take my phone from her baby hands, and now I'm forced to look at the notifications. I assume the countless missed calls and unread texts have accumulated from Brian wanting to talk things out.

"Hey, girl," Brandi says, returning from work.

I didn't even hear her open the door. My head is in a fog. "Oh, hey," I reply but can't bring myself to ask how her night was.

Brandi gives me a sympathetic smile. "How are you

holding up?"

I try to smile back but fail. "I'm okay," I lie.

She joins me on the couch and gives me a warm hug. "You look horrible," Brandi says, softly.

It's been twelve days since I drove over to Brandi's place to show her my torn and fragile heart. Twelve long, depressing days since Brandi lent me her shoulder to sob on, but since then, I haven't wanted to talk. This is Brandi's way of pressuring me to open up. Up until now, she has been patient and given me the space I needed.

"So, anyway, I know… you probably know that Brian has been texting me." She goes on and says, "He told me you haven't been returning any of his calls or texts, and he wanted me to let you know he's sorry for going back on his word."

"I figured you guys have talked." I force myself to continue, "Okay, but I really think Clarissa is trying to get back together with Brian, and he doesn't realize what's happening. I just can't believe he lied to me. I thought your brother was over her, but now I'm not so sure."

"Yeah, you might be right… I mean, about the whole Clarissa wanting to get back with Brian, but I also know Clarissa's dad is an addict," she tells me. "He's been addicted to hard drugs pretty much his whole life. I guess, every now and then, Clarissa's dad will convince her he's clean, or he's trying to get help. Sometimes, her dad tells her he's currently in a program. Supposedly, her dad lies about those things so she will let him back into her life, but Clarissa just ends up getting disappointed over and over again. It's a never-ending cycle."

Wow, Brandi sure knew a lot about Clarissa's family drama. I guess this is probably what Brian wanted to explain to me.

"I get what you are saying," I tell Brandi. "But I still don't think it was right that Brian kept talking to her even after he told me it was going to stop."

"Yeah, my little brother can be a dumb-ass sometimes," she says. "Nothing I didn't know already!" Brandi kisses Genesis. "Oopsie! Auntie said a bad word, didn't she?"

I let out a little laugh, thankful my daughter didn't repeat what Brandi said. "Well, I don't think I can be with someone who is constantly talking to his ex," I mention. "I know some people couldn't care less who their boyfriend or girlfriend keeps in touch with, but I'm not one of those people."

Brandi shrugs. "I wish I had more advice for you. I really do. Things will work out. Just try to stay optimistic."

"I will do my best," I reply, but know only time will tell if what I say is true.

Sometimes, giving up is easier. At times, the best way to prevent a broken heart is to never put it on display in the first place. Many times, holding a grudge is like holding up a shield to protect my daughter and me from harm.

"Hey! How about I make a quick stop at your

favorite tea shop and pick you up one of those weird-looking green teas you like… with boba?" Brandi asks. She grabs her purse before I can answer. "A tea will make you feel better in no time!" she says and heads out the door.

Maybe Brandi is right. Maybe I should try to be more positive, or maybe all I need is some boba to make my boy troubles vanish. I let Genesis walk around the living room a little and decide to read Brian's endless text messages from the previous day.

"Eva, please call me back."

"Can we just talk for a minute?"

"I love you. Please text me."

"I'm really sorry I lied to you, Eva. Please forgive me."

"I miss you and Genesis so much."

"I will try to call you again tomorrow. Please pick up this time."

"I really want to talk to you."

"What can I do to make things right?"

"I feel terrible. Please, I only need a minute to explain."

"Baby, please call me."

Baby? Brian's never called me *Baby* before. I don't like it—reminded me how Liam liked to call me Babe.

It's a good possibility Brian might actually really miss me. Maybe it was beneficial I let him hang out to dry for the last couple weeks. Clarissa must not be keeping him warm at night if he's been texting and calling me twenty times a day.

Yeah, that's right—keep thinking positive thoughts, Eva. I inhale deeply and sit up a little straighter. I start to respond to his texts and type: *"I miss you too, and I love you, but I'm nervous you will end up leaving me and Genesis like Liam did."* I reread the text and delete it, ignoring Brian… again.

My positivity quickly disappears.

As I scramble eggs in a pan for Genesis, I can't help but think of Brian's amazing breakfasts. I really do miss him, but what was left of my optimism has completely drained from my body.

Realistically, even married couples can't seem to make their relationships work. People leave each other for the dumbest stuff. One day, boyfriends and girlfriends will tell each other how much they love one another, and then the next day, they say the most damaging things. Vows are taken for granted. People cheat like there won't be any consequences. I no longer have any more positive thoughts to spare, but who can blame me? This is reality.

"Okay! One matcha tea with boba!" Brandi says, enthusiastically as she walks through the door. "And one black tea for Max, whenever he decides to get his lazy butt out of bed."

"Thank you, Brandi," I say and take a sip of my tea.

"How is it? Do you feel better?" she asks.

I smile at her and nod. "Yeah, so much better," I say while chewing on the delicious tapioca pearls. I feel my worries begin to hibernate, and my mind begins to focus only on the delicious boba.

This is when I realized *food is a form of momentary euphoria.*

"I'm so glad it's finally my weekend!" Brandi says as she grabs Genesis from her highchair and swings her around. "I've missed this pretty lady so much!"

Brandi holds my daughter in a tight embrace and kisses her. She sets Genesis down in front of the TV, and I slump onto my couch bed again.

"What do you want to do after I take a nap?" Brandi asks.

I'm too down in the dumps to *want* to do anything. "I was just thinking about staying in," I explain.

"What? No, you can't do that," Brandi says, disappointed. "You should get out of the house. It will be good for Genesis and you," she suggests.

"I mean, I was planning on watching movies with Genesis," I say.

"That's it?" Brandi places her hands on her hips, annoyed.

"Well… and eat the entire tub of cookie dough ice cream in the freezer."

"You can watch a movie any other night when I'm at

work, and Max already ate all the ice cream yesterday."

"Oh, that's lame. Max didn't even save me a little?" I say, bummed.

"Seriously! Let's go out!" she demands.

Brandi will not ease up. "Well, maybe we can go get some ice cream or something?" I ask.

"Oh, my gosh, Eva! That's like a two-minute outing. You had better come up with something when I get up from my nap!" Brandi shouts and heads to her room.

I try to think of excuses to mope around the townhome as I hear Brandi becoming restless. Max is gaming hard next to me before he leaves for work.

Eventually, Brandi walks into the living room and asks, "So! What's the plan?"

"Uh, well… I've actually been wanting to upload my paintings. I want to put them up for sale."

Brandi looks confused. "Okayyy…" she replies.

"I was thinking you could spend some time with Genesis, and I could get my gallery set up online."

Now she looks frustrated. "Ugh! Eva! Fine! I will watch Genesis, but I'm only giving you an hour. After that, I'm taking you out to dinner. I've been dying to try that new sushi place that just opened up down the street."

I sigh. "All right, but… then ice cream after?" I ask, hopeful.

"Yeah, ice cream after," Brandi confirms.

Max pulls off his headset. "You are going to sell your

paintings? I thought you were planning on hanging those masterpieces up in the townhome," he says, bummed.

"Don't worry Max," I say. "If no one buys them, then you can have them. So, there's a good chance you will get your wish."

His facial expression looks sympathetic, and he gives me a side hug before grabbing a snack and heading to the hospital.

I had completed a handful of paintings since Valentine's Day. As I sit in front of the computer, I think of how Brian's encouragement motivated me. His kind words pushed me to attempt to do something I love, but I can't help but feel hesitant putting my paintings on display for the world to see—not sure they will meet anyone's expectations.

"Without risk, there is no reward," I say to myself. Personal pep talks tend to help once in a while. I look at Genesis hanging onto Brandi's hand and think of how I need to be a good example for my daughter. How will I be able to tell her to follow her dreams if I never follow mine?

Chapter Twelve

Brian Ryan

The San Diego sun rises higher, and it revamps the saddened sapphire sky into brilliant shades of amethyst and ruby. Clouds begin to emerge, and the palm trees are no longer silhouettes in the distance.

Typically, I would have never noticed the harbor sky during a work night, but ever since Eva walked out of my life, my world has done a one-eighty. It's not the same without her.

The cool wind gently rocks the vessel as we begin to escort a five-thousand-passenger cruise ship into dock. I pull my phone out of my pocket and think of texting Eva for the hundredth time this week. Instead, I scroll through a handful of photos of Eva and Genesis. I miss their smiles and even more, their laughter.

"You good over there, Ryan?" Officer Butler asks, sitting in the cabin.

I slide my phone back into my pocket and reply, "Uh, yeah. I'm good."

"Eva?" Butler asks.

I rub my tired eyes. "Yeah, man. She won't return any of my calls or texts. It's been about two weeks since we've spoken."

"Ah, don't fret too much, buddy," Butler says. "Every now and then when I piss off my wife, she ignores me too." He chuckles. "She eventually gives in because she can only go so many days without a foot rub."

"I don't know, man," I say. "I think I really messed things up."

We notice a sailboat a few hundred yards away, floating in the path of the cruise ship. Butler gives the jets more throttle. As we approach the boat, he shouts at the driver through the PA system and orders him to clear the channel.

The skipper acknowledges his command and Butler continues on with his advice, "Just give her some time. She'll come around eventually. Over the years, I've learned that women like to hold grudges. It's in their genes. They just can't seem to let things go like us men."

"I hope you are right," I say, still doubtful. It seems like it's been months since I've talked to Eva, but only weeks have passed.

We finally arrive at the cruise ship terminal and

watch as the ship comes to rest against the dock. I try to focus on my surroundings, but it's no use. Eva is on my mind. Ever since the day I saw her in that lingerie, she's all I ever think about. I wish she knew that. I wish she knew Clarissa just needs someone to lean on, and nothing's going on between the two of us.

Speaking of my ex... I swipe my finger along my phone screen.

"Hey, Clarissa," I say.

Her voice is muffled, and I can barely understand her words through her uneven breathing and sniffles.

"What's going on?" I ask.

"Would you be able to stop by today?" she asks.

"Uh, yeah. I will be off work in a couple of hours," I say. "I can head over then."

"Okay, I really need you… I really need to talk to you."

I stand at the front door of Clarissa's apartment. The same place we created years of memories. Crap, maybe this is a bad idea. If Eva knew I came to see Clarissa, she would probably be even more upset with me. I don't want to ruin any chances I have getting back with Eva.

Rather than continuing to debate what's right and wrong, I ring the doorbell, assuming Clarissa heard some bad news about her dad. Maybe he was arrested for the second time this year.

Clarissa opens the door and greets me with a hug.

"Hey, Brian!" she says. Her demeanor is completely different than how it was on the phone earlier.

"Oh, uh, hi," I say, surprised and walk into the apartment. "Are you doing okay?"

"Oh yeah, I'm good," she says and chuckles. "I was just having a little breakdown this morning."

"So, you don't need to talk?" I ask as I look over my shoulder. I could easily turn toward the door and leave… I think.

"Well, I do want to talk," she says, and I notice her face looks a little different than it usually does.

"Are you wearing makeup?" I ask, confused.

The only time I remember Clarissa consistently wearing makeup was when we first started dating. Then, when I asked her to be exclusive, Clarissa only dolled herself up on special occasions. Once we moved in with each other, she abandoned putting in the effort altogether.

Clarissa giggles. "I thought I would try something a little different today," she explains.

She tucks a strand of hair behind her ear, which isn't tied back in her typical ponytail. I stare at the ends of her hair grazing the top of her freckled shoulders.

"Here, I made you a cup of coffee," Clarissa says, handing me a hot mug.

"Thanks," I respond and take a sip.

The brew tastes weak, and again, I think of Eva. I've grown accustomed to the strong Vietnamese coffee due to the constant tea runs I made for her. This cup doesn't compare.

"I figured you would be tired from working all night," Clarissa says. She grabs my hand and guides me to sit down on her couch.

"What did you want to talk about?" I ask. "Did something happen with you and your dad?"

"Well, not exactly. I actually want to talk about *us*."

I smell the fragrance of Clarissa's perfume—the fragrance she only wore on our yearly anniversaries. Then, Clarissa adjusts the thin strap on her shirt, and I notice her lack of clothing. Clarissa hasn't changed out of her silky pajamas—the ones she knows were my favorite because they were almost see-through. Shit.

I inch myself farther away from Clarissa, but she scoots closer, diminishing the gap between us. I focus on drinking my coffee, but Clarissa touches my chin and forces me to turn my head like a puppet. I have no choice but to look into her eyes. Clarissa's not nearly as beautiful as Eva, but she is familiar, and her presence is still satisfying after being apart for almost a year.

"Over the last few months, I've realized how much I miss being with you," she says warmly.

"Damn. Eva was right," I say quietly to myself.

"What's that?" Clarissa asks.

"Uh, nothing," I try to hand her back my half-empty coffee cup. "I came over thinking you needed to talk to someone about your dad. I should probably get going."

Clarissa puts one of her hands on top of my thigh, which is dangerously close to my package and refuses to take my cup.

"Brian, don't you miss being with me too?" she asks.

I gently remove Clarissa's hand from my leg, hoping that answers her question.

"We can start over, or… we can pick up where we left off. If you want to get married, I will sincerely consider it," she says.

"Clarissa, I wanted to be here for you if you needed someone to talk to, but I don't think I can do this anymore. Not if I want things to work out with Eva… and wait, what? No! Even if I wasn't with Eva, we couldn't just pick up where we left off."

"You have got to be joking me," she says. Clarissa begins to pace back and forth across the room. I guess she still does this when she's pissed. "Eve? You love Eve!" She continues to fume. "I can't believe this!" she yells. Clarissa looks like someone who is going through a manic episode. "We started dating in high school. That's like eleven years together! You started seeing Eve just months ago, and now you want to blow our relationship on your sister's best friend? This is bullshit! Did you hear me, Brian? Bull… shit!"

She finally waits for me to say something. "Her name is Eva," I mention.

"Oh, whatever!" Clarissa screams.

I think I've made her more angry because I corrected

her, so I try to deescalate the situation. "I'm sorry, Clarissa. I don't know what to tell you. If you had made your mind up a year ago things would probably be—"

"I'm still in love with you. I will always love you, and I know you love me too!" she says.

I decide not responding is the best solution to Clarissa's assumption about my feelings. Luckily, after a few more laps around the apartment, Clarissa finally starts to calm down.

I feel like a horrible person hurting Clarissa, but I know where my priorities lie. They lie with Eva and Genesis.

If I'm ever going to get out of this place, I think now is a prime time for me to leave since Clarissa isn't screaming my ears off. I walk to the kitchen to set down my cup in the sink, but unfortunately Clarissa corners me.

"Are you still in love with me?" she asks, sternly.

I don't respond again, but it looks like Clarissa has something else to get off her chest, so I let her speak out of pity before pushing past her.

"Come on, Brian, just answer my one question, please."

In hopes of Clarissa letting me leave, I answer her question and try to be as blunt as I can with her. "You know you will always mean something to me, but we can't be together."

"Why not?" she asks, pleading. "Please, Brian. I can be whatever you want me to be. Just give me another chance."

Clarissa! You were always so stubborn. Some things don't change.

"Come on! What do you want me to say? Yes, I love Eva, okay!" I shout. "I want to be with Eva!" I lose my temper and scream into Clarissa's face. She throws her hands over her eyes and begins to cry uncontrollably.

"How could you say that to me?" Clarissa murmurs.

"Oh, come on!" I yell, frustrated, but it's difficult to watch Clarissa cry. I let down my guard and hold her in my arms. "I'm sorry," I tell her. Clarissa looks up at me, and I stare into her big, green eyes.

"Please take me back, Brian. I wish we would've gotten married. I really do love you. I've never loved anyone like I love you."

Holding Clarissa in my arms reminds me of dancing with her at our high school prom. Her dolled up face makes me think of good times. The scent of her perfume sends me back to better days with someone I thought I would spend the rest of my life with. Clarissa's body pressed against mine, combined with her outfit, brings me back to long intimate nights in the bedroom. I am tempted.

"Clarissa…" I say, and she begins to raise herself onto her tiptoes. Her eyes are closed, and I lean in. My eyes begin to shut as well, but then I'm blinded by a vision of Eva and Genesis. I quickly let go of Clarissa and say, "I don't think we should talk anymore." I become agitated, thinking of how long I've allowed Clarissa to attempt to seduce me into getting back together with her. "Don't call or text. I won't respond," I tell her firmly and walk to the front door.

I look over my shoulder and see Clarissa scrunched up into a ball on the kitchen floor. I inhale deeply. "Goodbye, Clarissa."

Chapter Thirteen

Doubletake

"I need to change Genesis' diaper," I say to Liam as I walk into his house.

"Oh, I got it," he says and takes our daughter from my arms.

I smile warmly at Liam before he walks away. I can't believe this is the *new* Liam. The Liam who wasn't capable of washing his own laundry is now changing diapers. It's insane to think how he is actually becoming a great dad.

I set down Genesis' baby bag, and when I look up, I realize Liam had decorated his living room walls with paintings—my paintings. For a moment, my lungs have difficulty filling themselves with air, and my heart feels like it has taken a break from beating. Why would Liam buy my paintings?

I hear Genesis' baby giggles as Liam brings her nearer. I even think I might've heard her say dada just now.

"Liam—you… my paintings. I thought—" My words are lost somewhere in my chest. I point to the painting of the Hotel Del, and he grins.

"They are amazing," Liam says. "I bragged to my parents about your other hidden talent when they came over the other day. They were impressed by your artwork."

"I thought some stranger bought my paintings," I say. I force myself to take a deep breath, and I turn toward Liam. "But… why?"

Genesis reaches for her toys, and Liam sets her on the floor so she can enjoy herself. I realize she is becoming even more comfortable spending time with her dad.

"Why did I buy them?" Liam asks.

I nod, still surprised.

"I wanted to show you that I support your painting endeavors."

"Oh, all right, but you really didn't need to do that," I respond.

"Plus, they are a great addition to my home," Liam adds.

I'm not sure I believe him because the three paintings are so different from one another. Besides the one of the Hotel Del, there's one of a lonely tree on a cliff and another that is a palate painting of fruit. It probably would look better if Liam hung the paintings in different rooms. I wonder if he displayed them in the living room so I could see he bought them. It would make sense because Liam has never given up on anything easily… Well, except for his daughter and me—temporarily.

"Uh, I mean"—I shake my head—"thank you. I really appreciate it."

"Of course," he says and wraps his arms around my shoulders. I let him linger closer than I normally would. "I have a lot of apologizing to do."

"I already told you I forgive you," I say.

"I know, and I'm extremely thankful. Now, if only I could forgive myself."

I wrap my arms around Liam, and he holds me tighter than he's ever held me before. Too many days have gone by since I've been hugged by a man. I feel Liam kiss the top of my head and then he whispers, "I am still in love with you, Eva."

I can't help myself, and I look up at Liam. I am vulnerable and the wound in my heart, which was created by Brian, is yearning to be stitched up. Negativity fills my bones as I think of Brian spending time with Clarissa. Terrible thoughts of Brian and I never getting back together impair my decisions.

Am I selfish to find comfort in Liam's arms? Is it wrong that I'm allowing myself to fall for his genuine words? Is it possible I can find happiness beside Liam?

"I swear, I will never let you and Genesis go, ever again," Liam says while turning to look at our daughter, and I see his sincerity. "I want us to be a family."

I am unable to form words and continue to stare into his eyes.

"I know I have a long journey ahead to earn your trust back, but I'm willing to do whatever it takes—however long it may take. You girls will be my top priority for as long as I breathe."

I continue to believe every word falling from his lips.

"Uh, I—" I stammer, unable to express my muddled feelings.

I have no chance to recollect myself because Liam has pressed his mouth against mine. My mind is disputing, but my entire body feels like it's healing. The cracks in my heart begin to fill, but thoughts of Brian cloud my head. I am no longer lonely, but I still yearn for Brian's lips—I abruptly pull away.

"I'm sorry. I—I have to go," I say and run out the door.

No! What did I just do? I think to myself as I drive away. Tears begin to fall onto my face. Tears that are filled with guilt and confusion. The temporary stitches dissolve prematurely, and the wounds on my heart feel even worse. I look back at Genesis' empty car seat, and I feel more lonely than ever.

Chapter Fourteen

Words of Wisdom

"Everything tasting okay?" I ask Mr. and Mrs. Young.

"Yes, everything tastes just as good as it does every Wednesday," Mr. Young replies and takes another bite of his eggs Benedict.

"Are you doing okay, Dearie?" Mrs. Young asks me. "You don't seem as chipper as usual."

I force a smile on my face and lie, "I'm doing good, Mrs. Young."

"You look like one of those walkers on the *Walking Dead*," Mr. Young tells me.

I laugh. "You watch that show, Mr. Young?"

"You bet your bottom I do, but by myself." He points his thumb at his wife. "She's too big of a sissy."

His wife brushes off his comment. "Are you and

Brian doing all right?" Mrs. Young asks—always so sharp as a tack. "We are here if you need to talk."

I take a seat beside Mrs. Young. No formal invitation needed.

"So, Eva, what's the issue this time?" Mr. Young asks me.

"It's kind of a long story, but I will try to get to the point," I tell Mr. and Mrs. Young.

"We've got a lifetime. Spill it," Mr. Young says.

I explain to Mr. and Mrs. Young my predicament with Brian and Clarissa, along with my assumption that Clarissa is trying to find a way back into Brian's life.

"Oh, dear," Mrs. Young says, touching her hand to her wrinkled cheek. "Did he tell you why Clarissa needed someone to talk to?"

I shake my head. "No, I didn't really ask."

Mrs. Young reminds me of Brian pleading for me to stay.

"Well, why the hell not?" Mr. Young asks.

My favorite customer reminds me of storming off and leaving without giving Brian a chance to explain himself.

"I don't know," I say, sadly. "I guess I was just so upset and was afraid of being left again."

Mrs. Young places her hand on my shoulder. "Aw, Eva. I can tell you really miss him."

I am reminded of my heartache.

"Yeah… I do, but there's also something else," I say,

hesitantly. "I may have… kissed Liam—or let Liam kiss me… the last time we saw each other… or something like that."

The elderly couple doesn't look surprised. Their expressions look more sympathetic if anything.

I manage to create a somber smile on my face. "So, do you guys have any advice for me?" I ask, hopeful.

"You need to go talk to that boy!" Mr. Young says, pointing his finger at me.

"But what about the whole thing with Liam?"

"Screw Liam!" Mr. Young says. "He had his chance!"

My eyes widen at Mr. Young's intensity. "Oh… okay," I reply.

"Yes, Dearie, Liam did have his chance," Mrs. Young agrees.

"All right, but I don't know how Brian will react to the fact that I kissed Liam."

"Eh, I laid it on one of Mrs. Young's girlfriends way back when… and the wife still stuck around," Mr. Young says.

My jaw is hanging wide open. "Uh, really?" I manage to ask, and once again, Mrs. Young slaps the back of her husband's head.

"Yes! And I will never forget that, you hussy," she says while glaring at Mr. Young.

"I didn't say it was justified," her husband responds and shrugs. "Thankfully, she forgave me. I would've been heartbroken the rest of my life if she hadn't taken me back."

I see Mrs. Young try to hide a smile. Then, she stares me straight in the eyes and says, "I'm glad I forgave him, but anywho, back to talking about communication. It is the most important aspect of a relationship. There's no way I would've been able to put up with my husband's lousy lovemaking all these years." Mrs. Young leans toward me and whispers, "I will let you in on a little secret… The wave does matter just as much as the size, Dearie." She sits upright again and winks at me.

Ah! Mrs. Young, she never fails at making my ears burn. Words like these should not be coming from a lady's mouth! Especially, a lady who is as old as Mrs. Young, but I've come to sort of expect it, so I guess I'm not completely in shock.

There isn't an ounce of shame on Mr. Young's face. "I'm resourceful and a fast learner," he says. "But if the ol' ball and chain didn't let me know what she wanted in bed, then I can't say she would've stayed with me for more than a year." I assume his joke is semi-true, or at least… I think he is joking.

The three of us have a good laugh. Mr. Young runs his hand through his wife's curly gray hair and gives her a peck on her cheek. I quickly leave their table to check on my other diners, knowing full well I had just witnessed Mr. and Mrs. Young's foreplay. Any minute now, they will be all over each other like two horny salmon fish that have just made it upstream to mate. It's quite an eyeful for the employees and other diners, but Janette hasn't and never will tell her best customers their PDA is too excessive.

As I attend to my other diners, I contemplate about Mr. and Mrs. Young's advice. They've never led me down the wrong road before.

The couple's lecture about "talking things out" remind me of Liam's lack of communication when he was upset. Liam usually just stormed off and ignored me whenever we got into an argument. Many times, Liam wouldn't talk to me for days, which is exactly what the Youngs had called me out for. I feel like such a hypocrite.

I notice Mr. and Mrs. Young have taken a break from sucking face and have finished eating their brunch. I make my way toward their table and confidently say, "I am going to take your advice and talk to Brian. If anyone knows how to build a long-lasting relationship, it's my favorite customers."

They both smile at me. "We are so glad to hear that, Dearie," Mrs. Young says.

I clear their table and bring them a slice of strawberry pie.

"Oh, what's this?" Mr. Young asks as I place the plate in front of the couple.

"I want to give you a slice of pie—my treat," I tell them.

"Oh, that's so sweet of you," Mrs. Young says,

already digging her fork into the crust.

"It's a thank you for all your words of wisdom and for taking the time to talk to me," I explain, happily.

Mrs. Young's finger guides a crumb off her lip and into her mouth. Then, she pats the booth, ordering me to sit down again. She waves her hands toward herself, telling me to come nearer. I scoot closer, she embraces me in her motherly arms, and says, "Any guy would be so lucky to have you and Genesis in his life."

Mr. Young scrapes the last bite of strawberry pie on his fork and feeds it to Mrs. Young. They share an intimate moment, smiling at one another. It warms my soul to see their plate empty and their hearts full.

Chapter Fifteen

Drunk on Brian

"Come on ladies!" Brandi yells in my face. "You guys are so… slow!" Her words are starting to become noticeably slurred. "I just want to make one last stop!" Brandi says and trails her index finger down the side of my face. I wince at Brandi's touch but try not to be a party-pooper and allow her to harass my face as she pleases. Brandi puckers her lips in an attempt to kiss me, but her body sways and she smooches the air. Her lipstick is smeared from wiping the various types of alcohol off her lips, and I am barely able to hold back my laughter.

Brandi finally gives up on doing weird, drunk things to my face and walks ahead of Michelle and me—leading us to another bar. The bride-to-be reminds me of a baby giraffe who just entered the world minutes ago. The reference reminds me of Brian carrying Genesis on his shoulders as they looked at the orangutans at the zoo. The memory reminds me of Brian kissing me passionately in front of all the people in the restaurant. I try to stop my mind from wandering too far and begin following behind Brandi. I stare at Brandi's stilettos that are attached to her long legs that continue to wobble, and now I'm convinced I haven't seen her this wasted before.

Brandi turns toward us and says, "Come on you… sluts!"

Apparently, Brandi is an impatient drunk.

Michelle speeds up—a professional at jogging in her pumps and glitzy black party dress.

"I can barely walk in this ridiculous outfit you made me wear, Brandi!" I shout loudly in hopes they will slow down for me.

Michelle is so sweet just like her brother. She ends up running back for me and grabs my hand to pull me along. "Let's go, Eva," Michelle says, excitedly. She's like a sexy Olympic sprinter, running back and forth on the downtown sidewalks. "You should have at least one drink before we leave," Michelle suggests and drags me into the bar.

I feel my temperature rise due to the number of warm bodies that are swarming around the bar and on the dance floor. Wait, is this a bar or a club? I look at the youthful people in front of the DJ and cringe watching them grind on one another.

Michelle and I find Brandi standing at the bar. "Drink up, bitches!" she says, handing us a shot glass filled with some type of clear alcohol. I don't really prefer the names Brandi is calling me tonight, but it's her bachelorette party. So, I guess it's fine.

I look down at the drink Brandi shoved into my hand. I begin to panic, thinking back to the first and last time I took a shot. Oh, gosh…

"You have to do it!" Brandi ordered me, on her 21st birthday. "And after you take a shot, I'm going to make you a long island iced tea. I've been watching some videos on YouTube. I think I can make you a pretty good one!"

For whatever reason, her parents allowed her to throw a boozy, pool party in their backyard. I looked around at the couple making out in the corner on Brandi's parents' outdoor swing and then at the girl in a thong bikini shaking her booty in front of some lucky guy.

"I mean, I don't *have* to," I told Brandi. "I think your other guests have consumed plenty of alcohol for the both of us."

I feared losing my inhibitions. I wasn't sure how I would react. Would I be a happy drunk? Would I be an angry drunk? Would I want to pretend to be an exotic dancer and shake my butt in some guy's face like that one stripper-girl over there?

"Just down it—real fast," she instructed. "I promise, it only burns, like, a little."

Unlike Brandi, I couldn't qualify as an underage drinker. One time when I was twelve, I snuck a sip of my dad's whiskey. It felt like my throat was on fire. So, ever since then, I have been afraid of adult beverages.

"I don't know..." I said and stared at the shot glass, intimidated.

Brandi guided the glass to my lips, and I unwillingly opened my mouth. I tried to swallow the entire shot all at once like I had seen people do in the movies. I quickly removed the glass from my mouth, not able to take the full shot. I tried to swallow the liquid that burned my mouth, but again, flames crawled down my throat. The remaining vodka in my glass sloshed onto the ground as I bent over to try to control my coughing. I ended up vomiting a second later, and I blamed it on my full stomach—*not my novice drinking skills.*

"I think I just ate too much of my mom's fried rice before I came over," I announced. All of Brandi's guests were laughing and pointing fingers at my throw-up that reeked of meat and rice.

"Ah, sorry, Eva," Brandi said, cringing at the mess I made in her backyard.

Ugh! That was a terrible day, to say the least.

I set the glass down on the bar. "You do remember what happened the last time you made me take a shot, don't you?" I ask, trying to remind Brandi of the horrific event at her party.

"Oh, pfff! That was a long time ago," Brandi says, waving her hand a little too close to my face. "Read the sash," she tells me and points to the bridal ribbon that hangs over her shoulder. "It says…" Brandi fails at reading the words that are upside down. "It says, you have to do what I say tonight because *I… am… the… bride.*"

I shake my head. "No, Brandi. Your sash doesn't say that."

Brandi holds her arms above her head and announces loudly, "Yup! Everyone hear that? I'm going to be married. Come and get er' boys!"

A few older guys wearing business attire whistle at the bride-to-be.

"All right, Brandi. Let's just take it down a notch," I say.

"Loosen up a little, Eva!" Brandi yells and forces the shot into my hand again. "Now, drink up, you dirty whore!"

"Brandi, stop calling me mean names," I say. I think I sound exactly like a kindergartener on a playground who is being bullied.

She ignores me. "Cheers to me!" Brandi shouts.

Michelle joins Brandi and holds up her shot glass. Fine! What the heck? I clink my glass against theirs, giving in to their peer pressure. I cross my fingers and pray I don't throw up all over the bar.

"Oh, no! It burns! It burns!" I scream. Brandi and Michelle are both laughing hard, specifically at me.

"You got down the whole shot this time!" Brandi says, enthusiastically. "I'm sooo proud of you."

I nod my head, unable to produce real sounds because of my scorched throat. I sit down on the stool beside me as the fire slowly extinguishes in my body.

"You want to dance? I want to dance! Let's go dance!" Brandi says to Michelle, pulling her toward the dance floor.

My head starts to feel fuzzy, and my body becomes relaxed. I'm embarrassed to admit this, but I think this might be my first buzz. I remember my mom telling me she is allergic to alcohol. She mentioned something about our Asian bodies not being able to filter the alcohol properly or something like that.

"Hi, there." I hear a voice in my ear. I turn my head and notice a cute, skinny boy has approached me. He adjusts his square-frame glasses before awkwardly holding his hand out for me to shake.

"Uh, hi," I say, taken by surprise.

I slowly bring my hand up to shake his. The boy's hand is sweaty, and I bluntly attempt to wipe the moisture off my hand. My palm misses the bottom of my dress and accidentally glides along my bare thigh. Disgusting! Damn you, Brandi, for pressuring me to buy this revealing party dress. Such a bad influence. Now I just rubbed this boy's sweat into my skin.

The nerdy guy glances back at his group of college buddies standing around a table a few feet away from us. I see one of his goofy friends give him a thumbs-up, and I giggle at their optimism.

"Hi, um, I'm Josh," the boy says and fondles the row of buttons on his shirt. He kind of reminds me of someone I might've dated when I was in high school.

"Hi, Josh. Nice to meet you." I shoot him a friendly smile. "I'm Eva. You and your buddies having a nice time tonight?" I ask and wave at his friends.

They pretend they don't see me.

"Nice to meet you too. Um, yes, we are enjoying our night out." Josh pulls a stool over next to me, sits down, and says, "So, um, you must have eleven protons because you are sodium *finnne*!"

What the…? "Uh, sorry, what was that?" I ask, confused.

"Oh—" Josh chuckles to himself. "Just a joke. Nothing… really… So, can I buy you a drink?"

"Um, no I'm okay. Thank you though."

"Please, let me just buy you one drink. My friends don't think I can pick up a girl as attractive as you," Josh begs.

I check out his table of friends again and see them passing some kind of blue and yellow playing cards amongst themselves. The cards look like they have a red and white ball on one side. I assume those are what they wagered one another.

"Ah, looks like they already think I don't have a chance," Josh tells me and starts to slowly slide off the stool. "Well, have a nice night. It was a pleasure meeting—"

I feel sorry for Josh, and I could use the company. So, I abruptly grab his arm and say, "You know what? I would love a drink."

"Really?" Josh asks, excitedly. "Okay, what can I buy you?"

"Yeah, I guess I will have whatever you're going to have," I tell him and smile.

We turn to face the bar, and he flags down the bartender. "We each will have one sex on the beach."

"Oh, sex on the beach?" I ask him, confused. I'm thankful Josh didn't order us straight whiskey or vodka.

"Yeah," he shrugs. "My friends give me a bunch of crap when I order girly drinks, but I like the fruity flavors. Also, what most people would consider *manly* drinks burn my throat."

"I agree one-hundred percent," I say. Josh is unintentionally hilarious. "All right, well, I'm not much of a drinker, and I have never had sex on the beach before," I admit.

"You mean you never had *a* sex on the beach before?"

"Oh, yeah. What did I say?" Josh laughs and looks pretty comfortable around me now.

The bartender places the tropical-looking drinks in front of us. "Oh, it looks so pretty," I say, eyeing the orange on the rim and cherry floating on the ice. I eagerly take a sip. "Ooo, I like it, Josh!" I say and eagerly take another drink. "It's really tasty! Good pick. I can see why you like it so much."

"I'm glad you are enjoying my drink of choice. I have other drink recommendations too," he tells me.

"If your other recommendations are as good as this one, you should definitely keep them coming." I begin to feel even more relaxed, and the warmth in my body starts to branch out.

"Do you also like pineapple and coconut?" Josh asks.

"Heck yes, I do!" I say, excited for my first ever extended alcohol experience. I was so deprived during my college years. "I can't believe I've missed out on all these delicious drinks!" I demolish my first cocktail and start on the next.

"Oh, my gosh! This pina colada is so slushy! I love it! It's like an adult Slurpee," I say.

Josh chuckles. "So, how old are you?"

"Didn't your mom ever tell you to never ask a woman her age?" I ask, sarcastically. Josh looks embarrassed, thinking he might've offended me. I slap him on his shoulder! "I'm just messing with you. I will be twenty-nine this year," I tell him, shamelessly.

Josh looks surprised. "Well, you sure don't look twenty-nine. Hold on… uh, so you are twenty-nine and you've never had a pina colada before?"

"Nope!" I say, deeply gulping down my cocktail. "Parents were super overprotective, and I never wanted to disappoint them. Oh, and I've had some bad experiences with drinking. I also think I might be allergic to alcohol," I explain. "And, yeah, Asians have like super freaky genetics that makes them look ten years younger than they really are." I use both of my hands to frame the sides of my face and then the top and bottom—such awkward, unnecessary motions, and now I'm positive I am drunk.

I finish my delicious slushy in less than three minutes. "Ah! Brain freeze!" I yell as my face scrunches up in pain. I recover and grab Josh's drink that is still half-full. "You don't mind, right?" I ask and continue to gulp down the last of his alcoholic Slurpee. Josh looks slightly shocked but doesn't seem to mind.

I forcefully yank Josh toward the dance floor. "I feel like dancing!" I yell.

Josh doesn't put up a fight. "Uh, yeah, I guess so," he says.

I would have never been caught on a public dance floor if I was sober. I only ever danced in private when no one was looking. Whenever my mom or dad would walk in on me, I would stop mid-dance and pretend to be cleaning my room or something dumb like that.

I spot Brandi and Michelle in the middle of the dance floor and pull Josh next to them.

"Okay, I'm not a very good dancer," Josh tells me. His arms are plastered to his sides, and he looks like an inexperienced virgin about to get down and dirty.

"Don't worry. I've practiced a lot in front of the mirror," I say.

I place my hand on Josh's chest and slowly walk around him. I whip my hair behind my shoulder, thinking I might look as hot as an exotic dancer working a pole.

As the DJ starts to blast some song about two-steppin' and gettin' tipsy, I position myself in front of Josh's statue-esk body. I squat awkwardly in my scandalous dress after running my fingers from his upper body to the top of his pants. Then, I jump up, ejecting myself into the air like a jack-in-the-box. I almost knock Josh's glasses off in the process, but I continue to dance, unaware of my clumsiness.

"Oh, uh, I'm okay," Josh says, replying to my nonexistent apology.

"What was that?" I ask. "You like that?"

I ram my butt into Josh's crotch and attempt to back that *thang* up. Josh and everyone else who are lucky enough to witness my awesome dance moves probably think I'm suffering from some sort of nerve damage. I try to remember how the well-endowed girls dance in the music videos I used to secretly watch behind my parents' backs in middle school. My racy dance moves are super offbeat, to say the least. I have no idea what I'm doing, but it's fine because alcohol continues to course through my body.

I look over my shoulder and notice Josh isn't really dancing. He's just weirdly moving his arms in the air like an octopus underwater. I turn to face him and look at his shocked expression. "What's going on? Not enjoying yourself?" I ask while brushing my hair off my clammy forehead.

He gives his tentacle-like arms a break and says, "Uh, Eva. You are beautiful, and I—I am having a good time." I notice Josh's dark brown eyes as he speaks, and they remind me of Brian's. "But I think you might've had too much to drink."

I point to his friends, still standing at the table. Their jaws have dropped to the ground. "See your friends are enjoying the show!" I yell and wrap my arms around the top of his shoulders.

"Are you sure you are okay, Eva?" Josh asks.

"Kind of"—I shake my head—"I mean, yeah… I'm good!" I try to convince Josh.

I place my hands on the back of Josh's neck and force him to sway to the music as if a slow song is playing. "Uh, Eva." Josh uses his index finger to push his glasses up the bridge of his nose—I am making him uncomfortable. "Typically, you don't dance like this unless it's a slow—"

"Shh!" I say loudly as I aggressively press my finger on his lips. "Put your hands on my waist!" I demand.

"Um… Oh, okay," Josh says. He looks around embarrassed but does as he's told.

I look into Josh's eyes again. "Bria—Josh… you have the most gorgeous eyes."

The boy's youthful face begins to blur, and his glasses disappear.

"Brian, I've missed you so much," I say and lean my body against Josh's. My hands caress the sides of his face. "I want us to be together again." I position my hand on the back of Josh's head and bring him in closer for a passionate kiss.

Whatever the mind believes is real, and my mind is imagining Brian's experienced lips—not Josh's. It's envisioning my body wrapped in Brian's perfect physique—not some underweight college student's body. I see a man who continues to hold my heart in his hands—a man who I cannot stop thinking about. I am content being here with someone who treats my daughter as his own—not someone who doesn't know I'm a mother.

"Ah, Eva!" Michelle shouts, pulling me away from Josh. "Okay, I think it's time to get you girls home."

Brandi's arm is draped over Michelle's shoulder, and Michelle continues to yank me through the crowd.

I look over my shoulder and realize the guy I was kissing wasn't Brian after all. I enjoyed my make out session nonetheless and would give anything to kiss Brian one more time—real or fake Brian, either will do right this moment.

"I don't want to leave yet," I whine. "I'm having so much fun! Did you see that guy I was grinding with? I still look like I'm nineteen!"

Minutes later, I find myself sitting in the backseat of an Uber. I pull out my phone from my clutch and fumble with it as I try to unlock the screen.

"Dammit. Where's his number? I know I didn't delete it," I say aloud to myself.

"What are you talking about, Eva?" Brandi asks, sitting next to me.

"I'm going to call… Prince Eric," I tell her.

"Huh? No, you are most definitely not!" she yells and grabs the phone from my hand.

Michelle looks over her shoulder from the front seat. "Prince Eric?" she asks.

"Yeah, he still has the most dreamy eyes, and the perfect teeth," I say. "I just want to chitty chatty with him for a minute."

"You and alcohol do *not* mix well," Michelle says while shaking her head.

I attempt to grab my phone out of Brandi's hand. "Ah! Nope!" She shoves my phone under her butt. "Not happening."

"If you want to make a phone call it should be to my brother… well, when you are sober," Brandi says.

"Brian doesn't want me. He wants his *darling* Clarissa." I showcase two thumbs-down and make an obnoxious fart sound with my mouth.

"Oh, just stop, Eva," Brandi says.

"What? And Dr. Ken said I can call him if I ever need anything… *anything at all*," I mention. "That's *exactly* what he told me."

Brandi rolls her eyes. "Fine, Eva. Do whatever you want. I drank too much and can't deal with this sort of thing right now. You are literally a buzzkill," she says and tosses my phone onto my lap.

I find Ken's contact info and… blackout—unaware of what came next.

The following morning, I find myself lying down on Brandi's couch with a throbbing headache. Brandi hands me a glass of water and a bowl of oatmeal.

"My favorite hangover food," she tells me.

"How are you even functioning right now?" I ask, rubbing my temples.

"I recover better, and I at least have a small tolerance to alcohol, unlike you."

"Oh, my gosh, Brandi. Never again. Never!" I say, looking at my dress I had apparently been in the entire night.

She laughs at me and says, "I think you had yourself a good time last night, making out with that adorable, nerdy college dude! I thought you were going to rip off that guy's clothes after showing him a good time on the dance floor."

"Ugh, please don't remind me," I say while I think back to my strange dance moves and make out session. I guess I shouldn't have given Brian such a hard time about his dance skills.

"You were really tearing it up last night with those stripper moves of yours," Brandi mentions.

I roll my eyes at her comment.

"I also heard you call that guy Brian," she reminds me.

I inhale deeply. "Yeah, I can't believe I did that. I really miss Brian, Brandi."

"I know you do. That's why I didn't think it was a good idea for you to call Dr. Ken last night."

I frantically reach for my phone. "Oh, my gosh!" I shout.

"Oh, you don't remember?" Brandi asks.

"You let me drunk dial Ken?" I fumble trying to bring up my call log. "No, no, no. Please, tell me I didn't do that."

Brandi laughs. "No, you didn't. You ended up deleting his number, and then you fell asleep."

I fall back onto the couch in relief. "Thank God."

"It was a close call though. I really thought you were going to go for it," Brandi says.

"I don't know what I was thinking," I reply.

"I know… the alcohol was doing the thinking for you," Brandi chuckles.

"I can *officially* say that I'm allergic to alcohol."

"I know. I could tell by… what do they call it? You had a certain Asian glow last night."

I glare at Brandi. "I did not!"

"You so did, and last night was so much better than

my 21st birthday party!" Brandi slaps her thigh as she dies from laughter.

I grumble. "Oh, whatever."

"Oh, gosh, Eva." She wipes the tears from her eyes. "I'm only kidding! Anyway, you should go over to Brian's today and talk to him while your parents still have Genesis," she suggests.

I take another bite of my hangover remedy and begin to feel better. I can feel the sustenance restoring my mind and strengthening my body. After I scrape the bowl clean, I feel like myself again. I thought, for sure, nothing besides time would help subdue my hangover. Food is so much more than just… *sustenance.*

This is when I learned *food is a form of healing.*

Chapter Sixteen

Forgive or Not to Forgive

Genesis clings onto my neck as I stand in front of Brian's condo. "Brian, I'm sorry for not answering your texts or returning your calls. I shouldn't have ignored you and given you a chance to explain," I say to myself, practicing my speech for the fourth time today. I fill my lungs with air, release my breath slowly, and ring the doorbell.

Brian answers the door in his underwear, reminding me of what I've really been missing out on the last month. It seems I woke him up from his sleep, so I begin to apologize for my timing. "I'm sorry. I didn't mean to interrupt—"

Brian cuts me off and embraces me and my daughter in his arms. "I've missed you girls," he says softly, still holding us tightly.

"I'm sorry for not answering your texts or returning your—"

Brian cuts me off a second time and grabs my wrist to guide us inside. "Don't apologize, Eva. I should be the one saying sorry. You were right."

"I was right?" I ask, confused. "Right about what?"

"You were right about everything," he replies, and I realize he means I was right about Clarissa's intentions. "I officially told Clarissa I'm done. I can't sacrifice my relationship with you for the sake of my ex's needs."

Brian must have been practicing his speech too. Genesis eagerly reaches for Brian to hold her, and he willingly accepts her instruction. Genesis nestles her head in Brian's chest and my heart is content. Apparently, I'm not the only one who yearned for Brian's love and affection.

"I'm sorry I walked out on you without letting you explain first," I tell Brian, admitting I was wrong. "I need to tell you about something, though," I say as he sets Genesis on the ground.

I sigh, preparing myself for the worst and begin my confession, "The last time I dropped off Genesis at—"

"You don't need to explain anything. I love you so much, Eva. I wasn't sure how I was going to manage another day without you and Genesis." Brian pulls me in close and kisses me for the first time in a month—one of the longest months we had ever endured.

I slide my arms underneath Brian's and reach behind him to feel his broad shoulders. I've missed his warm embrace and his addicting lips. I squeeze myself against Brian's chest, urging him to kiss me longer, but then guilt presents itself. I forcefully push myself away from Brian.

"I kissed Liam!" I scream.

"What?" he asks, shocked.

"I mean. He kissed me, but—but I… let him… kiss me," I admit.

Brian sits down on his couch, and his eyes begin to wander around the room. He is stunned and in disbelief.

"I'm sorry, Brian." I stand still like a statue, afraid of making a wrong move. Brian slumps over with his hands over his face, and I try to explain, "I've been feeling like a complete and utter hypocrite. I—I… missed you, and I didn't know what was happening between Liam and me. I mean… I did, but he—I didn't mean for it to happen." My practice speeches went a lot smoother—much less stuttering and stumbling over my words.

Brian uncovers his face and looks at me sadly. "Do you still love him?" Hope is slowly draining from Brian.

I swallow the lump in my throat. Okay, Eva. Be honest, don't lie, and most importantly communicate.

"Liam will always have a piece of my heart," I say. Moisture fills my eyes, and I see Brian start to crumble.

"No," Brian murmurs as he holds his hands to his face, trying to cover the tears falling from his eyes.

I slowly walk toward him and say, "But Liam had his

chance, and I will never be able to love him again like I used to. I will never be able to love Liam… like I love you."

I pause in front of Brian, unsure of how this is going to end because this is the first time I've ever seen him cry. This is the first time I've devastated Mr. Right.

"I'm so sorry, Brian. I know I can't make up for what I did. I know that loneliness and vulnerability are never excuses."

I give him a minute to recollect himself. Brian's crying ceases, but he doesn't respond. He just stares at Genesis walking toward him. She places her hand on his knee. Genesis isn't smiling. She looks like she's trying to console him, but Brian looks like his mind is adrift—my words have paralyzed him, and I begin to think he will never forgive me.

"Please, say something," I plead. "I don't love Liam."

Still no response.

I don't want to give up on our relationship, but I am also fully aware of my betrayal. I don't know what else to say to make things right.

"Okay, I should go," I say and reach for Genesis.

Brian takes a deep breath. "No, stay," he says and grabs my arm. I freeze in place, but Brian doesn't release his grip. I assume Brian is waiting for confirmation before he lets go.

I nod, and Brian picks up Genesis. He quickly hugs me, and says, "You are still my favorite girls."

And now my heart is fully mended.

Chapter Seventeen

Worth It

Brian wanted me to stop by with Genesis again the day after we made up. We both needed each other after all the drama and time spent apart. Obviously, we have missed each other's company.

Brian cut his sleep short a couple hours early to spend time with me, and Genesis has been napping for a little while. So, here I am again… making out with Brian on his couch… and really showing him how much I've missed him. I notice Brian briefly slide his head next to mine, and I can tell he is looking over my shoulder at the time on his watch.

"Time flies when you're having fun," Brian says.

"I know you have to go to work soon," I say, looking into his eyes. "You know… you could play hooky, and I could make you a nice dinner." I can tell by the expression on Brian's face that my persuasive words are making an impact. "Then, after we put Genesis to bed, we can have some alone time. I *need* you, Brian."

Brian grins. "Ah! Eva!" He's weighing his options.

"I promise it will be worth it," I mention as I straddle him on the couch. I begin to kiss him for a moment for more enticement. "So, what do you think? You think you should *work* from home tonight?" I ask.

"All right, I have a lot of time saved up. I think I can make it happen."

I smile at Brian's decision and give him a peck on the cheek before heading to the kitchen to make a home-cooked meal for my deprived lover.

"Wait! I thought you said you were going to make it worthwhile!" he shouts.

"I said after Genesis goes to bed!" I laugh.

"Come on, Genesis is still asleep," he says and follows me into the kitchen.

I smirk and change the subject because if I give Brian what he wants now, what's stopping him from going to work tonight? I want every minute I can get with Brian.

"So, did you get next Sunday off for Brandi's wedding rehearsal?" I ask while pouring soy sauce into a pot on the stove.

For a moment I am thankful we had resolved our issues before the wedding shenanigans. How awkward would it have been if we hadn't worked things out?

"Oh, yeah. I did. I was able to take a personal day," he tells me. "So, anyway! Eva, that reminds me. I also saw some pictures on Brandi's social media from her wild bachelorette party. Looks like you ladies had a productive Friday night."

I think back to drunk kissing that nerdy college boy. I think his name was, Josh? I felt like I should tell Brian about that kiss too. I definitely intended to bring it up. Guilt sinks into my stomach again. My confession regarding Liam's kiss had taken priority over Josh's.

"I meant to tell you something else too, Brian. I kissed a guy at a bar—at a club," I stutter. "I mean, somewhere downtown," I say, quickly—just like ripping off a band-aid.

"Oh, are you talking about this guy?" Brian mentions as he pulls out his phone.

"Huh?" I ask, confused.

The room is overwhelmed by Brian's laughter as he begins watching a video. I hear the club music playing in the background, and I realize he's watching a video from Brandi's bachelorette party.

"Wait, what? Oh, no! Brandi wouldn't!" I say in a panic, hoping Brandi didn't put me on display on social media.

Brian proceeds to play the video of my drunken self, using a poor, scrawny boy as a plaything on the dance floor. I cringe from embarrassment.

"Yeah, I don't think I'm too worried about that kid," Brian says. "But you've been holding back on me, Eva."

"I didn't even realize Brandi was recording that!" I shout.

I grab the phone out of Brian's hand, and I'm relieved to see Brandi hadn't posted the video for the public to see. She sent her brother the video Saturday morning with a caption that read: *"Your girl is a hot commodity. Look at those dance moves! You'd better figure things out quick before someone else scoops her up!"*

"Apparently, if you give me a couple of drinks, you can have your very own private lap dance too," I joke, trying to poke fun at myself.

"I think I might have a couple of beers in the fridge," Brian says, sounding a little too serious.

I shake my head and return to the kitchen to give my teriyaki sauce one last stir before I turn off the burner. "Never again!" I say and chuckle to myself. "So, anyway!" I willingly change the subject again. "I put my paintings up for sale online."

"You did?" Brian says, excitedly. "I'm really proud of you. People are going to buy those things like crazy."

I instantly regret switching the subject, remembering Liam had already bought three of them, but I also think back to Mr. and Mrs. Young lecturing me about communication. I don't want to keep anything from Brian.

"Oh, so, I did sell some… already," I say, hesitantly.

"That's great!" Brian replies, excitedly.

I pause from cooking and look at Brian.

"I don't know about that. Uh, so, Liam actually bought… three of… my paintings," I say.

I cringe thinking about what's going through Brian's head. He looks pissed for a few seconds and then says, "That's it! How much do you want for the rest of your paintings? I want to buy all of them. Right now. Tell me the price!"

"Oh, my gosh," I respond and roll my eyes.

"I'm not about to let your ex make me look bad," he says. Brian is a little too serious about purchasing my artwork.

"I'm not a gold-digger," I reassure Brian. "No one can buy my love."

If that was the case, I would be with Dr. Ken.

I throw some chicken into a plastic bag to marinate in the teriyaki sauce, and Brian walks over, inhaling the sweet and savory air. "I missed you almost as much as I missed your cooking," he says, tickling the sides of my ribcage.

I flinch at his jabs. "Stop! You are going to make me ruin dinner," I say, trying to pour the remaining sauce into the bag. I missed our laughter, but even more, I missed showing my love for Brian through food.

Chapter Eighteen

Noodle Trap

I slide Genesis into a cute sundress, and then I text Liam. *"Just a reminder... I won't be dropping Genesis off until after Brandi's rehearsal."*

Liam texts me back: *"No problem, Babe."*

Liam calling me "Babe" kind of worries me. We haven't talked about the last time I was at his house when we kissed. I mean, right after the whole… "mistake" and running out on him, Liam did text me and asked if I was okay. I replied that I was fine, which wasn't really true. I hope Liam doesn't think we are on a path to patching up our relationship.

"You girls about ready to head out?" Brian asks.

"Yeah! Genesis is ready to practice her flower girl stroll," I reply, excitedly.

I grab the bouquet I made Brandi, created from the ribbons and bows I collected from her engagement gifts. They made the perfect “mock bouquet” for her rehearsal. Supposedly, the ribbon bouquet is put together for good luck. I made sure to provide a red bow to ensure the luck was even more legit since the color red in Chinese culture symbolizes happiness, success, and good fortune.

As I buckle Genesis into her car seat, I ask Brian, “Can you believe your sister is getting married?”

“It’s pretty crazy,” he replies. “I’m glad she found Max—someone who can put up with her for more than a week.”

“Oh, gosh,” I reply as I slide into the passenger seat. “All of those guys Brandi dated before Max were the worst. They might’ve been attractive, but they treated her like crap. Those guys could never have been Brandi’s Mr. Right.”

Brian shrugs and points at himself. “I’m a sexy man. I treat you like crap, and you’re still with me.” He grins. “Are you sure I’m still *your* Mr. Right?”

I shove Brian’s shoulder. “Just quit it. You do not. If anything, you treat me like a queen,” I say. “You will always be my Mr. Right.”

“If you say so,” Brian says, jokingly.

“Stop fishing for compliments,” I laugh.

“Hey, I take what I can get,” he says, sarcastically.

I think back to when I was thirteen, and my mom found a list I made inside my jewelry box.

It read:

Mr. Right

tall, but not too tall
not bald
~~*solid eight pack*~~ *abs like Tarzan*
perfect smile
dreamy eyes
will help around the house
good sense of humor
adventurous like Aladdin
~~*likes*~~ *loves food*
good listener
likes to watch movies

"I read the list you made," my mom said as she set a bowl of fried rice in front of me.

"Huh?" I replied, not sure what she was referring to.

"All the traits you are hoping for in your… what did you write? Oh, yes, *Mr. Right*," she said while grinning.

My eyeballs bulged from my skull. "Oh, my gosh, Mom! That was supposed to be private!" I shouted across the dinner table.

"I'm sorry, Hunny. I was just looking for one of my bracelets. I thought it might've gotten into your jewelry box somehow."

"Well, you didn't have to read it!"

She chuckled. "I couldn't help myself." My face was probably ten shades of red. "There were a lot of physical traits toward the top of your list," my mom mentioned.

"Ugh! They aren't in order," I explained.

"How come you don't want Mr. Right to be loaded?" my dad asked.

"Oh, my gosh! You read it too?" I yelled. My face was scrunched up in annoyance.

"No, Hunny. I just told him about it," my mom replied.

"Same thing," I said and crossed my arms, frustrated.

"I thought it was cute. I don't know why you are so upset," my mom said.

"I don't want to talk about it anymore," I said, like a normal moody teenager.

Apparently, my thirteen-year-old self was pretty smart. I feel like Brian met a lot of my criteria.

"What are you thinking about?" Brian asks as we pull into the venue's parking lot.

I shake my head and smile. "Oh, nothing."

"Wow, Brandi! Your venue is unbelievable!" I tell her. The place Brandi had chosen for her ceremony is nothing more than ideal for Max and her—the perfect beach wedding.

I eye the hundreds of boats that line the marina before beginning our walkthrough of the ceremony. The turquoise waters are calm, and Genesis runs on the leafy green grass, briefly distracted by a couple birds soaring through the sunshine in the sky. I notice Brian run toward Genesis. He swoops her up and spins Genesis around. Sweet giggles leave her body.

"I know, it really is beautiful, isn't it?" Brandi says, and then dramatically breathes in the crisp air. "So, Eva, you will be walking with Max's best man, Greg." Brandi waves him over. "He's Max's cousin."

"Nice to meet you, Greg," I say, holding my hand out for a proper greeting.

Greg's the most gorgeous red-headed man I've ever seen, and he has piercing green eyes. His smile is charming, and I start to assume he's probably as great of a guy as Max.

"Well, well. What do we have here?" Greg says, and then he kisses the top of my hand. Apparently, this gesture *isn't* found only in movies.

"Ew, Greg!" Brandi yells, "Do you have to be such a pig? She's already taken!" She angrily points to her brother a few feet away from us. Thankfully, Brian is still happily distracted, playing with Genesis.

"I'm only being friendly," Greg says.

I laugh, assuming Greg's just messing around, but I wipe the back of my hand on my shirt because who knows where his mouth has been. I decide I incorrectly judged Greg and suddenly, he doesn't look as handsome anymore. This guy seemed like a *certified* playboy.

After our formal greeting, Greg and I line up and wait for our turn to walk down the grassy aisle. I look over my shoulder at Brian holding Genesis' hands. Brian pulls out a few of the fake flower petals he had sprinkled on his floor inside the love fort, months ago.

"Our turn, Eva," Greg says, tugging me along on his arm. As my feet slide across the grass in my flip-flops, I wonder if I should've worn my bridesmaid shoes to practice walking in. I can barely walk in heels on solid ground and the "rough" terrain worries me. The rest of Brandi's and Max's wedding party take their places beside Greg and me, and now we patiently wait for my daughter to make her way down the aisle.

"Come on, Genesis, you're up. Let's go, little lady," Brian says from a distance. Genesis does *not* want to cooperate. Instead, she twists her body in the opposite direction as Brian attempts to pull her toward us. Brian hands her a couple of petals, but Genesis tries to shove one into her mouth. Everyone chuckles at my adorable daughter. Brian gives up about halfway down the aisle and carries Genesis the rest of the way.

Finally, I see Brandi at a distance, and she is holding the bouquet I made. I feel myself holding back tears, and now I am confident I will be a complete wreck on the actual wedding day.

*****

My phone vibrates in my purse while Brian pulls his truck out onto the road. Liam had text me: *"I decided to sit down and eat lunch at the Noodle House. Would you mind dropping Genesis off at the restaurant?"*

"Hey, so I just read a text from Liam," I tell Brian. "I guess he's eating lunch at a restaurant. Do you think you can take us there instead?"

"Yeah, that's not a problem," Brian replies.

"Okay, but you still have to wait inside the truck. You can't go inside with me," I say, reminding him *those* plans have not changed. One of my goals is to still keep Liam and Brian at a distance during our exchanges. I feel like it's more important now than ever since the whole kissing incident. I can tell from Brian's expression he doesn't want to wait in the truck.

We pull into the Noodle House's parking lot. As I take Genesis out of Brian's truck, I look at the outside of the restaurant, and it reminds me of Liam and my monthly dates. I picture us happily indulging ourselves in a massive bowl of ramen.

"I will be just a minute," I assure Brian. His lips are pinched tightly together, and Brian props his elbow onto the window and rubs his chin. I can tell by his body language he really does not want me to drop off Genesis by myself. I guess I'd better hurry. "It won't take long," I say.

Brian just nods, frustrated.

I find Liam sitting at a table inside the restaurant, but there's not just one bowl of noodles in front of him. "Hey, Babe. Just in time," he tells me.

I put Genesis in her highchair, not processing what Liam had just told me, *or* the second bowl of steamy ramen, *or* the fact that he just called me Babe. I'm focused on a quick exchange, so I don't keep Brian waiting.

"I ordered you lunch," Liam mentions. Then, he stands up from the table and kisses my cheek. I flinch and take a step away from the table. "I thought we could talk more about what happened between us the other day," Liam says.

"Oh, uh, thanks," I say, surprised. "But I actually don't have time to sit down and eat right now. I'm already late to lunch with Brandi and the rest of the wedding party."

"Oh, I see," Liam says, disappointed. "You know you could just sit down for a minute and take the ramen to-go."

"Liam, I really can't," I say, becoming worried about Brian barging into the restaurant.

"Hi there," the server says. "Is everything okay?"

I look around, and the people seated at the nearby tables are staring at Liam and me. "We are fine. Thank you, though," I reply.

She gives me a stern look and says, "Well, just let me know if you three need anything."

I nod my head and wait until the server is a few feet

away from us before I speak. I try to talk more quietly and say, "Liam, I'm sorry. I shouldn't have let you kiss me. I—I wasn't thinking clearly." Liam and I are still standing beside the table, and Genesis notices the food she isn't being offered. "Please, I don't want to have this conversation here," I plead. More sets of eyes are beginning to make their way over due to my crying daughter.

I sit down and Liam follows my lead. I hurriedly tear open the chopsticks and notice Liam's shocked demeanor. "Hold on. So, you are saying… you didn't want to kiss me?" he asks.

"I was really upset at the time. I was confused. Okay, Liam. I'm sorry." I quickly break the chopsticks and brush off the ends onto the floor. Genesis' crying ceases as I place some noodles and veggies in front of her. I look at my phone and realize Brian has been sitting in the car for over five minutes. "Listen, I really have to go. I didn't drive myself," I explain.

I place my hands on the edge of the table in front of me. As I'm about to scoot my chair away from the table, Liam leans over and grabs the side of my forearm. I don't need to look around at the diners to know the entire restaurant is fixated on us.

"What's going on here?" Brian asks, sharply. My eyes shoot up, and I see Brian standing beside Genesis.

Liam releases my arm and stands up to address Brian. "Eva and I were just talking and having lunch,"

Liam tells Brian, angrily.

I look at Brian and shake my head. "We aren't having lunch. I was just trying to leave."

"Trying?" Brian asks.

"I mean… about to leave. I was just about to leave," I say, selecting a different choice of words.

Brian glares at Liam and says, "Well, I did just witness you physically *try* to keep my girlfriend from leaving the table. So, I think *trying* is the correct statement in this case."

I attempt to get some words in unsuccessfully. "Brian, it's okay. Let's just get out—"

"Don't worry, Eva. It's fine. I caught the end part of your guys' conversation too," Brian says, but still continues to look at Liam. Brian has a passive-aggressive smirk strewn across his face.

I am actually thankful I don't have to explain myself to Brian. If he hadn't heard some of Liam's and my conversation, Brian could've assumed the worse. Liam and I sitting at a table with food in front of both of us *definitely* looks like a lunch date.

Liam is fuming, and he takes a step toward Brian. Please, not again! I think to myself. Then, I see Liam's heels start to rise off the floor. This is so ridiculous.

"Eva said she's ready to go. She's got *other* plans," Brian says through his teeth.

"You know what!" Liam says, a little too loudly. "I've had about enough of your—" He looks at Genesis.

"Man, if my daughter wasn't sitting here…" Now Liam's practically an inch away from Brian's face, but Brian hasn't faltered the slightest bit.

I roll my eyes at Liam's ridiculous macho talk. "Liam," I say, trying to get his attention, but Liam and Brian continue to have an awkward stare down.

"Excuse me, you guys are disturbing the customers," the server says as she approaches Liam and Brian. The server's hands are placed on her hips, and she looks back and forth at the two men causing a scene.

They ignore her. Instead, Brian says, "Just calm down, buddy. I'm just going to take Eva and go. You can enjoy your lunch with Genesis, but you really need to get over the fact that you lost your chance. Eva is with me now."

"I think you guys better leave," the server says, loudly.

"We were just on our way out!" I reply and quickly grab Brian's hand.

"Yup. We are leaving," Brian says. He allows me to guide him out the door, but Liam and him can't seem to end their stupid staring contest—not until Brian and I make it outside.

"What a douche bag," Brian comments, and we hop into the truck. "What else happened in there, Eva?" Brian asks as he starts the ignition.

"I asked you to stay and wait in the truck!" I say, angrily.

"I did wait, and I waited some more," Brian says. "You were in there for fifteen minutes. You said you would be quick."

"I mean… it was more like ten minutes, but still!" I reply.

"I was worried, and it was a good thing I went in to check on you. Liam wasn't going to let you leave."

"I had it under control," I reply, confidently.

Brian looks over at me and then shakes his head. "Okay, Eva. If you say so."

"What? I did!"

Brian looks at me in disbelief.

I sigh. "All right, fine, so maybe I couldn't get him to listen to me," I say.

"Uh-huh," Brian responds.

"But Liam and I haven't really talked after… you know. After the whole—"

"Yeah, I know. I figured."

I'm thankful Brian filled in the blanks. I didn't want to have to say it out loud. I still feel terrible.

"At least Liam knows *now* that we won't be getting back together," I say and awkwardly smile.

Brian looks over at me but shakes his head again. "Oh, Eva," he says. I think Brian's just glad the whole "restaurant scene" is done and over with, and so am I.

"I'm sorry you had to deal with that," I mention.

Brian finally smiles. "Come here!" he shouts and wraps his arm around my shoulders. "I would put up with all the craziness in the world for Genesis and you. You know that," he says.

I'm relieved Brian's tension is rapidly vanishing. I turn the volume up on the radio, "Do you like this song?"

"Uh, yeah. I like *Boys Like Girls*," he replies.

We are silent as the background guitar serenades us, and a country singer's angelic voice accompanies the lead vocals. "This would be the perfect song to dance to at a wedding, don't you think?" I ask Brian, grabbing his hand off his lap.

Brian puts his truck in park but leaves the engine running, allowing the song to continue playing. I look at Brandi and the wedding party sitting by the window inside the restaurant as I unbuckle my seat belt. Brian doesn't care that we are late. He places his finger under my chin and slowly leans toward me. I can feel his breath on my lips, and they are begging for mine.

"You want this song to play at our wedding?" he asks before kissing me.

My heart misses a beat, goosebumps make their way across my skin, and my eyes close. I allow myself to become lost in Brian's words and the lyrics that are playing. Each kiss satisfies me, and Brian's love for me leaves me breathless. My mind makes me believe I'm sitting in paradise, falling even harder for this perfect man of mine.

"I see you two in there!" Brandi screams while pounding on the truck's window. I jump in my seat and pull away from Brian to see what all the commotion is about. Brandi's standing with her hand on her hip, and she's holding up the other pointing her finger at us. She continues to yell from outside of the truck. "Get your horny butts in the restaurant, right now!"

"You know, we don't have to listen to that lunatic out there," Brian says. Brandi looks even more annoyed now that we are both laughing.

"Seriously! Everyone's vomiting in there from seeing you guys going at it. No one wants to watch your little make out session!"

Brian unbuckles his seat belt and scoots closer to me. He grabs my head and forces his lips on mine, but I can barely kiss him back through my laughter.

"Guys!" Brandi screams. "Guys… Seriously! You are both so lame."

Out of the corner of my eye, I see Brandi walk back into the restaurant, defeated.

Chapter Nineteen

Final Day

"You ready to become Mrs. Martin?" I ask Brandi while walking through the glass door onto the balcony. Brandi's gaze transfers from the brilliant view from our hotel room to me. As Brandi smiles, I notice she has that typical bridal glow people talk about.

"I'm so ready," she says.

"Not an ounce of doubt?" I ask. "No wedding jitters?"

"Wow, Eva, are you *trying* to make me nervous?" she asks, sarcastically.

We chuckle. "I guess you are right. I don't know why I asked that. Everyone knows you and Max are perfect for each other."

I give her a side hug, and she leans her head against

mine for a moment. Brandi continues to sip on her coffee and enjoy the coastal landscape.

"What should we do for breakfast?" Brandi asks.

"Oh! I already took care of it. I ordered room service for all three of us," I explain.

Brandi and I accompany Michelle on the couch as trays and trays of food are brought into our room.

"What did you do, Eva?" Brandi asks. "Did you order one of everything off the menu?"

"It's a good possibility." I bite my bottom lip, worried I may have overdone it. "It all sounded so good. I had a hard time narrowing it down," I say through my laughter. "And I didn't want you to be hungry since you will be busy getting ready all day."

Michelle and Brandi are already indulging themselves in the copious amounts of food. "See, I knew I didn't order too much," I tell them and snag a bite of the Benedict before it vanishes.

"You most certainly did *not* order too much," Michelle tells me as she chomps down on a piece of bagel that's smothered in a thick layer of strawberry cream cheese. "You have officially made my morning with your crazed menu ordering."

"Yeah, I guess I agree with Michelle," Brandi says. "But this is why I love you so much, Eva. I never go hungry when you are around."

*****

A few hours later we are accompanied by Julie and Grandma Rose. Brandi and I stand in front of the vanity, looking at our bridal makeup and fancy hairdos.

"You look amazing. Max is going to cry like a little baby when he sees you," I tell Brandi.

"He'd better! It took long enough for me to look this good," she jokes.

"*All* of you girls look beautiful," Brandi's mom says.

Brandi heads toward the bedroom and grabs her dress from the closet. I notice Brandi's mom and grandma are prematurely ruining their mascara, unable to control their happy waterworks. I help Brandi step into her alluring wedding gown and slide each button into their loop along the back of her dress. As Brandi looks over her shoulder to pose for the photographer, I successfully hold back my tears. I step away from Brandi, so the photographer can snap endless pictures of the magnificent bride.

My mom brings Genesis into the hotel room, and my heart melts at the sight of my daughter in her blush-pink tutu dress. The top of Genesis' dress matches the lace on Brandi's wedding dress—intentional and adorable.

"Come here, my beautiful girl!" I tell Genesis and pick her up. My daughter stares at my face slightly frightened—unsure of who I am. I am temporarily unrecognizable due to the layers of foundation and powder. "It's okay, Genesis. It's Mommy," I say, and she smiles at the sound of my familiar voice.

My mom glances at my revealing bridesmaid dress and says, "You know what your dad is going to tell you when he sees you in that dress you are wearing."

I laugh. "Yeah, Mom. I know."

Grandma Rose feels the need to put in her two cents and says, "See, Eva, I told you."

I try to avoid rolling my eyes and focus on my perfect daughter I hold in my arms.

The moment has finally arrived. Brandi and Max are about to become husband and wife! The hundreds of guests gather on the lawn overlooking the marina, and the wedding party is lingering on the sidewalk behind a cluster of palm trees—away from the crowd.

"Eva, you have to tell me the truth," Greg says. "How serious are you and Brian?"

I look at Greg for a second and chuckle. "Pretty serious," I respond and look over at Brian holding Genesis. They are my everything.

My daughter is grasping the ribbon that is attached to a ball made of various shades of pink roses. This was one of Brandi's brilliant ideas to prevent my daughter from munching on flower petals. Brian seems to be keeping Genesis content by showing her a tropical flower on a nearby bush. Genesis hesitantly touches a bright petal with her fingers, abruptly retracts her hand, and giggles as she looks up at Brian.

I adjust my grip on Greg's arm, impatiently waiting for our cue, and for whatever reason, Max's cousin won't zip his damn lips.

"I call dibs if he crushes your heart," Greg says, obnoxiously. "Or vice versa." He nudges me.

Greg's the worst. I shake my head at his dumb words. "Shut up, Greg," I tell him, sharply.

"I'm only messing around, Eva. Jeez… Well, kind of." Greg looks smug, which is so annoying.

Thankfully, the song begins to play, which instructs Greg and me to begin our walk down the aisle. My dress feels so tight and super short. Even worse—the heels I'm currently wearing are impossible to walk in.

I awkwardly hang onto Greg's elbow and attempt to use him as support as I struggle to walk in a straight line along the grass. Greg tries to shift his weight to help steady me, but after a few steps, my ankle gives out—contorting in abnormal ways. Greg watches my hand slide off his arm, and the next steps I take, in an attempt to catch myself, cause my pointy heel to dig into the earth like a stake. Everyone's eyes are fixated on me as I unsuccessfully try to lift my heel out of the ground.

"Let me help you," says a stranger sitting in an aisle seat.

"No! No! I got it," I shout and bend over to grasp my ankle with both my hands. I grip my leg like I'm in a tug-of-war match and give my leg a solid pull.

"Crap," Greg says, witnessing me become off

balance a second time. I guess I shouldn't have yanked so hard on my ankle.

I hear my mom's voice somewhere in the crowd while my short legs take long strides to catch myself from face planting. "Oh, no, Hunny," she says, worried.

As if aerating the lawn with my footwear wasn't bad enough, I almost run into one of the rose pillars lining the aisle. My cheeks are becoming more and more flushed by the second as I hear the crowd wincing at my embarrassment. Finally, I gain control over my body and stop it from thrashing down the aisle.

"Shit, Eva. Can't you walk?" Greg says while making his way toward me.

I pause for a brief moment so I can figure out how to walk in these ridiculous shoes. I look toward the alter and notice we have barely made it halfway down the aisle. I hunch over with my hands placed on the top of my knees like a runner who just finished a marathon. I try to catch my breath, and then Greg decides it's a good idea to stand me upright by positioning himself behind me and lifting me from my armpits.

"Ah! Don't, Greg!" My whole body reacts in defense and wriggles like a fish. "Don't touch my armpits!" I say, loudly, and during that moment, I wished the music was blasting a little harder. I wished I had remembered to bring my pair of shoes to the rehearsal. More importantly, I wish Greg hadn't put his hands on my armpits! That is the one place off-limits to everyone and anyone!

"Stop being so stubborn," Greg whispers into my ear. "And walk on the balls of your feet."

I regain my composure, place a fake smile on my face, and attempt to finish my walk of shame. Dammit! My ankle hurts so bad! It reminds me of when that weird hippie stomped on my foot that one time at the sub shop but way worse. After taking another step, I feel my heel start to sink in again, and I quickly transfer my weight to the front of my feet like Greg instructed. Huh, I guess Greg knew what he was talking about after all. I wonder how he knew that would work. Always a groomsman, never a groom?

I'm grateful I was able to make it to the altar without another mishap. Next down the aisle is Brandi's mom, and she's pulling Sasuke on a leash toward us. I am grateful everyone is now distracted by the adorable, chubby wiener dog with the ring pillow strapped to his back. Surprisingly, Sasuke isn't attacking everyone in the crowd with his viciousness. I guess the wiener dog knows he's outnumbered, or maybe Sasuke doesn't mind because he's not at home. I giggle to myself as I watch the blades of grass scratch the underside of his large belly.

The pain from my ankle becomes non-existent as soon as I see the man of my dreams holding my daughter's hand. Hundreds of phones are out in the open, clicking away and taking pictures because Genesis is pulling everyone by their heartstrings.

Brian grins at me, and I know he is proud of

Genesis. He had been preparing Genesis for this day every chance he could get, and Brian's persistence has paid off. I'm no longer able to contain the moisture pooling in my eyes. This moment is perfect.

"Everyone, please stand for the bride," the pastor instructs.

Many of the guests are trying to peek around one another to get the first glance of Brandi—eager and impatient. Some are standing on their tiptoes, trying to get a full view while Brandi makes her way toward the love of her life. Everyone loves to watch the bride as she walks down the aisle, but my eyes are always drawn to the groom.

I stare at Max, who is dabbing the corner of his eyes with the back of his hand. I witness Max stroke his goatee as he longingly waits for his soon-to-be wife. I see Max swallow the lump in his throat that is caused from trying to hold back more joyful tears. I notice Max staring at Brandi like he has been waiting for her his entire life. The undeniable devotion Max has for Brandi is presenting itself in an exponential fashion.

Then, I notice one other person who isn't focused on the bride—Brian. He is staring at me from the front row, and I see him mouth the words, "I love you."

And I am hopeful, one day, *Brian* will look at me the same way Max is looking at Brandi.

The pastor begins telling a couple of beautiful stories about the bride and groom while they continue to hold one another's hands.

"Brandi told me about how she and Max first met," the pastor announces. "Online dating." The pastor nods his head multiple times. "God works in wonderous ways—" He holds his finger up to the Heavens and continues, "Even through the World Wide Web." He chuckles to himself and then quotes the Bible. "Mark 10:9, Therefore what God has joined together, let no one separate." The pastor says a short prayer and continues with the second story.

"The first time Brandi said those three special words to Max was when she took him indoor rock climbing. This was the first time Max had ever attempted to scale a wall. Max knew Brandi went rock climbing fairly often, and so Max was determined to give it his all. As Max struggled to make it just a few feet off the ground, his legs began to shake, and he was barely able to cling onto the holds, but at that moment… Brandi spoke those three special words—the three fulfilling words that define a marriage. 'Don't—give—up.'" A mixture of laughter and happy sobs surround the alter. "Well, not the three words I'm sure most of you were thinking," he says, turning the page in his book. The pastor pauses briefly, allowing our minds to process his words. Then, he goes on to quote the Bible again and says, "1 Corinthians 13:7, Love bears all things, believes all things, hopes all things, endures all things." He smiles warmly and looks at Max and then at Brandi. "There will be times when you disagree with one another. There will be times when you will want to ignore each other. There will be moments when you want to storm out of the house in the middle of an argument. Many times, you will want… *to give up*, but this is not what God wants for your marriage. God wants your love to *endure*. Don't—give—up."

Max pulls a tissue from the sleeve of his tux and wipes Brandi's tears. She grabs it from Max's hand and uses it to remove the snot dripping from her nose. Brandi chuckles and places the balled-up tissue back in Max's sleeve. I hear Greg say something about it being gross, and I desperately want to reach over and slap the annoying guy across the face.

"Now, for the vow exchange. The bride and groom have decided to write their own vows," the pastor announces. "Max, if you will go first."

Max continues to caress Brandi's hands in his. "What? You memorized your vows?" Brandi asks, surprised.

"No, I didn't spend hours and hours memorizing my vows," Max says, sarcastically. He squints at her. "I told you I was just going to wing it and say whatever comes to mind." Laughter fills the salty air and Max clears his throat before speaking. "Brandi Miu Ryan, I first want to thank you for putting up with my addiction. I wasn't sure how you were going to react when I told you I *need* to play Call of Duty on a daily basis. None of the other women I dated before you allowed me to game as much as you do."

Brandi slaps the side of Max's shoulder and then places it back in his hand. Who would've guessed that Max is just as much of a jokester as Brandi. "I promise to uphold our agreement… plus more. I promise you will never have to take out the trash as long as I'm able to. I vow to unclog the shower drain when your strands of hair clog it." Max chuckles, but then he becomes serious and continues, "I give you my word—to do whatever I can to make you happy, but most importantly… When we are wrinkly and our hair is gray, I promise to continue to love you the same as I do now but even more passionately. I vow to not only tell you I love you, every day for as long as I'm breathing, but show you. You will forever be the love of my life."

Brandi and Max give one another a peck, and Brandi runs her hand along Max's cheek. I don't think I've ever seen her this happy before.

"Brandi," the pastor says and nods at her, instructing her to speak.

She pulls her hands away from Max's. "I don't have as good of a memory as you," Brandi says to Max and pulls out a piece of paper from the inside of her bra.

"*Nicccce*," Greg says, quietly. I really want to punch him square in his nose.

"Max, I love you so much. You are not only everything I could've hoped for in a husband, but also in a friend. You love me when I'm at my best, and even after my craziest moments. I will, *definitely*, try my best to lessen those crazy moments as much as I can." Max smiles and shakes his head as if he likes that about Brandi.

I don't blame him. Brandi's craziness is what makes our friendship so interesting. It's a huge factor in why I call her my best friend. Life would be so bland without her spunky personality.

"I have to admit, when I first looked at your profile, I wasn't sure we would be compatible. When it asked for a favorite location, I put the beach, and you put GameStop. When it asked for favorite food, I put fried rice, and you put potato chips and gummy bears."

Max chortles, but I sincerely hope after eating some of my cooking, his favorites are no longer chips and candy.

Brandi continues, "For activities I put body surfing and rock climbing, you put… well we all know what you put." Brandi smiles at Max. "We might not look compatible on paper, but I know you are exactly what I have been looking for in a husband—in a soulmate. You are thoughtful and caring. You have the most selfless heart of any man I've ever known, and I can't wait to spend the rest of my life with you."

The chubby wiener is pulled toward the bride and groom as they say their I do's. Max and Brandi slide the rings onto each other's fingers. "You may kiss the bride!" the pastor shouts, happily.

Max dips Brandi over his knee. They kiss one another as a married couple for the very first time and cheers erupt. I hand Brandi her glorious bouquet of roses.

"Mr. and Mrs. Martin!" the pastor yells, and the newlyweds walk down the aisle one last time.

Greg jogs toward me. "Ah!" I scream as he picks me up. "What the hell are you doing?"

"Don't want to have another mishap with the lady who can't walk!" Greg announces to the crowd and carries me down the aisle.

"A little warning would've been nice," I say as I tightly squeeze my legs together. I tuck my hand under my butt just below my dress, so I don't give everyone a free show.

"This is how I would carry you into the bedroom," he whispers in my ear.

"You're a shit-bag," I tell him, angrily.

One of Brandi's aunties flinches at my words as we walk by. Whatever, it's fine. I'm pretty sure she's the only person who heard my name-calling.

Once we are out of sight and on solid ground, I begin to squirm. "Put me down, Greg!" I yell.

He does as I demand. "You're welcome," Greg says.

"You are so annoying!" I scream as I stomp off to get as far away from Greg as I can, but honestly, I am kind of thankful I didn't have to attempt to walk back on the grass in my heels.

I look at my parents, sitting a couple tables away

from Brian and me during the reception. Genesis clings onto her grandpa's jacket while my mom endlessly offers her food.

"This is good, but not as good as your food," Brian tells me and takes a bite of his salmon.

I brush my hand on the back of his neck, acknowledging his flattery. "I think Brandi and Max picked out a great caterer for their wedding," I say. "I think this is the best wedding food I've ever had."

"You know, I could watch some more cooking videos and learn how to cook some dishes like this… if that meant you would say yes to moving in with me," Brian mentions playfully, but I know he is probably serious.

"Hmm, is that so?" I ask, but then I'm distracted by the servers who have begun filling the champagne flutes. "Oh, I guess it's time for my speech," I say. "Give me the paper. Oh, and no champagne for me… tell them I want apple cider. We don't want a repeat of Brandi's bachelorette party."

"Huh?" Brian asks, taken by surprise at my abruptness.

"Oh, just give me the speech already," I say, anxiously.

"Uh, oh, okay," Brian says and pulls my written speech out of his pocket. I quickly grab the paper from his hand. "Wait, what about my question?" Brian asks.

I smile at him as I slide my chair away from the table.

"We'll figure it out," I say before walking toward the dance floor.

I yank at the hem of my dress as I think of Grandma Rose's not-so-kind words. I'm also terrible at speeches, so my heart starts to beat nervously. I've been practicing in front of Brian as much as he would let me, but the endless practice didn't help my nerves right this moment. I turn toward the crowd, and I see Brian giving me two, cheesy thumbs-up for encouragement.

I look over my shoulder at the newlyweds and try to remember I'm giving this speech for my best friend—my sister, and luckily it calms my anxiety a little.

The DJ hands me the microphone, and it screeches like in one of those lame rom-com movies. "Oh gosh," I say while laughing at my awkwardness. I notice my dad lean over toward my mom, and I assume he's probably telling her for the infinite time that I look like a hooch in my dress, which doesn't give me more confidence. Then, I see my baby girl clapping her hands, and my nerves completely disappear.

I inhale deeply. "Hi, everyone!" I say. "For those of you who don't know me, Brandi is my best friend—or more so, my sister. We've known each other since our freshman year of high school." I look back at Brandi again. Her hands are clasped under her chin, and happiness is radiating from her. "When I first met Brandi, I knew I had met someone with the biggest heart anyone could possibly have. We had multiple art classes together in high school, but the one class that is forever embedded in my brain is the art class we took our freshman year. This was actually the first time Brandi and I ever talked to each other," I explain. "I remember Mrs. Brown handing back our first art assignment, which was some type of oil pastel drawing. I remember turning over my drawing and almost having a heart attack. Mrs. Brown had given me a B-. Yeah, there was a big fat B- written in red pen on the back of my assignment. A large B-, just staring me straight in the face. I was so embarrassed. So, I did what any normal student would do, right? I quickly folded my drawing up and shoved it into my backpack. Thankfully, Brandi happened to be sitting next to me that day. It's funny now when I think back, but during that moment, I was so devastated I had received a bad grade. Brandi asked me if I was okay. She specifically said, word for word, 'You look like you are about to cry. Are you seriously upset about the B- Mrs. Brown gave you?' Okay… I might've been crying a little bit, in all honesty." I chuckle to myself. "I was really annoyed that this girl I didn't even know was giving me a hard time about my feelings. I had to explain to Brandi that a B- is like an F!"

I pause to look at my parents in the crowd and notice both of them nodding their heads in agreeance. I continue, "Brandi looked at me like I wasn't from this planet. She said, 'I'm pretty sure… a B- is a B- and an F is an F,' or something along those lines." Now my parents are shaking their heads back and forth, disagreeing with

Brandi's "naive" thoughts. "I told Brandi, 'You don't understand. I'm Chinese. Chinese parents consider anything less than an A- an F. So, therefore, I got an F on my assignment.'" Laughter rumbles throughout the room. "She mentioned that everyone has their own opinion about art, and that beauty is in the eye of the beholder. Now, I'm pretty sure there's certain criteria for art assignments, but there was also some logic to what Brandi was saying. There's always someone who will enjoy a piece of artwork even if a million others hate it. Anyway, Brandi asked if she could have my drawing. She wouldn't stop telling me how much she loved my artwork, and that Mrs. Brown must've been smoking something good. The next time I saw Brandi, she had folded my drawing into a cover for one of her schoolbooks. That's when I knew I had found someone worthy of a real friendship."

I feel all the warm fuzzy feelings coursing through my body, thinking about how much Brandi cares about me. "And it turned out I was right. Brandi stuck by my side through the hardest parts of my life. When I thought I had no one to help raise my daughter, she reminded me I had *her*. Many times, when I felt like life was too much, she helped me fight back." I hold back tears for the tenth time today. I turn to look at Max and say, "Max, you not only found someone who is absolutely stunning on the outside but someone with a heart of gold. You two are perfect for one another. There is not an ounce of doubt in my mind that you were meant for each other." Max smiles at me, thanking me for my genuine words. I point my finger at Max. "But Max, don't forget, I still need to teach you some more of my recipes. Might come in handy every now and then when Brandi drags you into the doghouse." I blow a kiss to Brandi before making my way back to Brian, relieved I didn't make a complete fool of myself like I did during the ceremony.

"You did a great job, Eva," Brian tells me as Greg readies himself for his best man speech.

I sit down beside Brian and notice Greg walking strangely toward the stage. "Wait, is Greg drunk already?" I ask Brian.

Brian shrugs and replies, "I guess we will find out." He laughs.

Greg's shoes awkwardly stick to the dance floor as he attempts to do the moonwalk. Then, the best man jumps, crosses his legs, and spins in place before speaking into the microphone. Everyone laughs… except me.

"Killed it," Greg says, breathing heavily.

"Yeah, he's, for sure, drunk," I say to myself.

"I'm Greg, Max's best man. Also, the best… *looking* man in the wedding party." Greg pinches his collar between his fingers and flicks it away from his collar bone. "Yeah, that's right," he says.

Greg turns around and walks toward Max, and he starts rubbing the groom's bald head. Greg continues on with his nonsense. "Not really sure how someone as 'good-looking' as Max… was able to wrangle a girl like

Brandi." Once again, laughter starts to fill the room. Mine is forever absent.

"Hey! Max is a handsome guy!" I try to yell, arguing with Greg, but no one can hear me except Brian.

"He's just joking around, Eva," Brian chuckles.

"That's what you think. He's so shallow," I mention.

I watch as Greg brings his hand up and points his finger toward Brian and me. Greg looks unsteady, and I wonder how many times he's visited the bar in the last hour. "And also, I haven't the slightest idea… how Brandi's little brother over there managed to find someone with such a fine ass as Eva's!"

"What the—" Brian says as he turns to look at me, shocked.

My eyes are wide, and my lips are pursed. "Uh—" I shrug with my hands up in the air. "Greg's been hitting on me," I tell Brian.

"How come you didn't say anything?" Brian asks, frustrated.

"I don't know," I reply. "I didn't think it was a big deal."

"Well, how long has this been going on?" he asks.

"Um… since Brandi introduced him to me," I respond.

"I could've taken care of it before it got out of hand," Brian says.

"But I thought things were good," I say. "I called him a shit-bag and everything, so I thought maybe I handled it."

"It's clear, he didn't take the hint," Brian replies.

Unfortunately, Greg is still rambling, and now I think he's reciting a poem to me.

"Roses are red, the sky is, uh… blue, I'd be your man, if Brian ever dumps you!" He looks around at the crowd, proudly, with his head held high. I think Greg is waiting to be praised for his lame poem, but no one applauds.

My mouth scrunches to one side of my face. "Yeah, apparently not," I say, looking at Brian.

"This guy is a douche bag," Brian says.

"I had a feeling you were going to say that," I reply.

Greg seems to be on a different inappropriate topic now. Something about… "banging out some babies."

"Eva and I would make the most gorgeous babies in the universe!" Greg shouts, lifting both his hands to the ceiling. Then Greg slams both his hands down onto his crotch area while doing frontal thrusts with his hips… repeatedly and says, "You know you want this, Eva!"

All eyes are on me for the time being. Thankfully, Brian's dad grabs Greg by his arm and drags him along the dance floor. Greg continues to chat away as Mr. Ryan pulls him toward the door. "What? I'm a sexy guy! I've got a gigantic sized—"

Luckily, Mr. Ryan gets the drunken lunatic outside just in time.

"Oh, my gosh," I say to Brian, unable to hold back

my uncomfortable laughter. "He is a psychotic drunk!"

Brian's no longer laughing. He looks pissed-off.

The DJ blasts another country song in an attempt to distract the guests. I see Brandi and Max chatting and then laugh. Fortunately, they aren't phased by Greg's inappropriate speech. The bride and groom probably expected something out of the ordinary from Greg.

Brian removes himself from the table to join his dad and Greg outside. "Where are you going?" I ask Brian, but he is already walking out the door.

My mom and dad walk over to where I'm sitting. Genesis is now happily hanging onto her grandma. As soon as I hold out my hands and offer to hold Genesis, my daughter nestles her head into my mother's chest—rejecting my offer. She must be having too much fun with her grandparents, like usual.

"And that's why you should wear more clothes, Daughter," My dad says. "Boys can't keep it in their pants."

"Oh, stop it! It wasn't the dress. It was the alcohol!" my mom says, countering my dad's assumption.

"I will be sure to keep that in mind," I say to my dad sarcastically and glance toward the exit. "Maybe I should go check on Brian," I tell my parents.

"Oh, no, Hunny. Just let the guys figure things out," my mom suggests.

I am relieved when I see Brian enter the room and

walk toward me, but then I notice Greg a few feet behind him.

"Greg wants to say something to you, Eva," Brian says.

Greg's eyes are focused on the ground as he approaches me. He looks like a child who has recently been released from a timeout—discouraged and apologetic. Greg glances up for a second. "Uh, Eva," he stammers and then begins to look around the room uncomfortably. "I, um… want to say sorry for being such a jerk."

"You should be ashamed of yourself!" my mom shouts at Greg. "This is no place for you to be performing your perverted dance moves."

Greg abruptly turns and walks away. I don't blame him. My mom probably would've ended up giving Greg even more of an earful.

"All right. Well, we don't have to worry about him anymore," Brian says.

"What'd you do? Threaten to knock his lights out?" my dad asks. "I would've."

"Dad!" I shout, shocked.

"Nah, Mr. Gin. I wouldn't do that," Brian says. "I just told him that Eva means a lot to me, and I would appreciate it if he treated her with more respect."

"You are such a good man," my mom tells Brian.

"Your dad tell that fool he'd knock his lights out?" my dad asks.

I've never heard my dad call someone a fool before, but I can also say that over the years, I have learned that most Asian parents are pretty protective of their children.

"Oh, my gosh, Dad. Really?" I say, but he doesn't acknowledge my comment.

"My dad sure looked like he wanted to punch his face in," Brian explains. "I think that was enough of an intimidation factor to get Greg to comply."

I catch my mom and dad smiling at one another. "Why are you guys looking at each other that way?" I ask them.

My mom leans over and whispers into my ear. "Your father and I really like Brian." She pats me on my back, and my parents head back to their table.

"So, really?" I ask Brian while Brandi and Max cut into their wedding cake. "It was that easy to convince Greg to cut the crap?"

"Uh-huh," Brian replies.

I don't know if I believe him, but I become distracted by Brandi smashing a slice of cake onto Max's face. Everyone is cracking up watching Brandi beg and plead for Max to preserve her lovely bridal face. Max doesn't spare his wife—showing Brandi what true love really is with cake and frosting.

"I have always thought it was weird that couples do that," I say to Brian.

"Huh? What's weird?"

"You know, the whole shoving cake into each other's faces at weddings," I explain. "It's kind of a waste of perfectly good cake. Although, I guess it's worth it for the guests' reactions."

"I actually think it's one of the best parts of the reception," Brian says, staring at his sister who is hysterically laughing.

Max feels bad and grabs a napkin to help wipe off the mess he created on his wife's nose. "No video games for you for the next… week!" Brandi yells, sarcastically.

"I might just skip the whole cake cutting thing if I ever get married. I'll just have the servers dish it up to the guests," I tell Brian.

Brian looks shocked. "What? No way! You have to. It's been a tradition since God knows how long. It's supposed to symbolize commitment."

"Did you just make that up?" I ask.

"What? You think I would make up something like that?" Brian jokes.

I stare at Brian with wide eyes. "Uh, yeah!" I reply.

"It's a fact. Trust me. I know these things." He seems pretty confident.

I swipe my finger along my phone. "Do you?" I ask, but Brian just chuckles while I search to confirm his so-called fact.

Hmm, turns out he was right. Who would've guessed?

*****

This is when I learned *food is a form of a promise.*

"So, did I change your mind?" Brian asks. "Are you going to smash some cake into my face?"

I entangle Brian in my arms. "Yeah, maybe," I reply, knowing full well that he one hundred percent changed my mind, and when that day comes, I will be fully committed to love him forever and always.

Chapter Twenty

Blue Heron

The sun is just beginning to hide itself behind the horizon, and Brian and I sit at our table as the DJ plays yet another country song. This time it's about a house party, which fits the current mood perfectly.

"Wow, Grandma Rose really knows how to tear it up on the dance floor," I mention to Brian as I watch her *very* slowly "raise the roof" and march around in a circle.

"Yeah, she's the one who taught me my dance moves," Brian replies.

"Ahhh, now it all makes sense. Well, at least she's enjoying herself," I say.

I notice my dad dancing with Genesis. He's holding onto her hands as she balances on the top of his shoes. I look at the empty tables and then at the full dance floor again. "Uh… So, do you want to dance?" I ask Brian.

"Do *you* want to dance?" he asks.

"Um… if you do. I will. I mean—we can," I say, slightly uncomfortable as I think of dancing in front of people.

"I don't want to embarrass you with my smooth moves," he says and smirks. Brian gulps down his last bit of champagne. "I have a better idea… How about we take a stroll along the marina? Doesn't that sound better?"

I nod my head. I'm glad *I* don't have to make a fool of myself. "That does sound like a better idea," I respond.

"Brandi and Max picked the perfect venue," I tell Brian. "The sunset is amazing."

He takes off his jacket and wraps it around my shoulders and says, "Eva, *you* are amazing."

Brian holds me close as the summer breeze rustles along the coast. Time stands still as we stroll along the marina's rocky edge. We pass a lonely heron perched on a large rock that is half-submerged in the water. The hundreds of boats sway gently, and the sun is just about to retire for the day.

Brian startles me slightly as he side-steps and quickly positions himself in front of me. "Oh, what's the matter?" I ask as my pace abruptly comes to a stop.

Brian caresses both of my hands and says, "I love you, Eva."

I smile. "I love you too," I reply. Brian clears his throat and swallows deeply as if he is nervous. "Are you all right?" I ask, impatiently waiting for an answer. Maybe he wants to make out for a few minutes. I don't really know.

Brian's eyes wander for a minute, and then he forces himself to look me in the eyes. He inhales deeply before responding. "No—Sorry, yeah, I'm fine." He shakes his head. "What I meant to say is, I undoubtedly love you, Eva… and Genesis. You girls mean everything to me. I don't think I could ever live without you or your perfect daughter."

I gently kiss his lips, but only for a second. I look up at Brian. "I know you do," I say.

"You make me so happy… The happiest I've ever been," he adds.

"Same here," I reply, but now I'm wondering where Brian is going with all this sweet talk of his. If he wanted to kiss me, I think he would've just done it by now.

Brian frees one of my hands and reaches into his pants' pocket.

"Oh, my gosh," I say quietly, anticipating what could fit perfectly inside a space that small.

My heart is treading through my chest at full speed. My breathing quickens, and I feel like I can't catch my breath as I witness Brian pull out a small box. He bends down on one knee, and my hands involuntarily cover my wide-open mouth.

"Eva, will you make me the happiest man on the planet?" he asks and begins to open the lid.

"Oh, my gosh, Brian!" I squeal, and there in the box lies… a key.

"Will you move in with me?" he asks.

My heart sinks into my stomach… but in a good way—I guess. I nod and smile while taking the box from Brian's hands. "Yeah, I will," I respond. Brian picks me up and spins us around.

When Brian finally sets me down, I ask, "Why did you do that?"

"Do what?" Brian asks, but he knows exactly what I'm referring to.

I glare at him. "You got down on your knee and everything!" I shout.

"Oh, you didn't think I was going to propose did you, Eva?" Brian asks, sarcastically.

I roll my eyes and entwine my arm around his, and we begin walking back to the reception room. "Well, that is typically what men do when they propose. You know, the whole one knee thing," I respond.

I search for my lone heron as we make our way back, but she's not on the rock any longer. She must have found a place to rest for the night, and I think of how they are solitary birds. I picture her asleep and alone in a tree. I squeeze Brian's arm a little tighter, grateful for the happiness he has brought me.

"Yeah, I guess you are right," Brian says. "It seemed

like you were getting pretty excited back there, and then you looked like you were a little let down because there was a key in the box."

I can't deny the fact that Brian read my feelings like a book.

"Anyway, the party should be clearing out pretty soon, and I think we should get Genesis home sooner rather than—wait, what's going on?" I say, confused.

I see Brandi, Max, and my parents standing outside the reception door. My daughter is fast asleep on my dad's shoulder, but everyone else is fixated on us. "Why are you guys standing outside?" I ask, but I only receive smiles and more stares.

Brian releases his arm from my grasp and faces me. "Eva Jade Gin—"

"Oh, my gosh, Brian," I interrupt. "You better not be messing around again!"

He chuckles and so does our audience. Brian positions himself onto his knee for the second time tonight and holds up a ring, pinched between his thumb and finger. "Will you make me the happiest man in the universe—"

"Yes! Yes! Yes! A thousand times, yes!" I shout.

I excitedly lunge at Brian and kiss him. It almost feels like the first time… but better. Brandi begins to hoot loudly into the night sky. I look over, and she's pumping her fists while jumping up and down.

"And just in case you are curious… this was all

Brandi's idea," Brian tells me.

"What do you mean?" I ask.

"Well, I kept telling my sister I didn't want to take away from her wedding day when she suggested I propose tonight," Brian explains.

Brandi chimes in, "I told him he had to, or I would disown him!"

Brian shakes his head. "She told me it would be the best wedding present anyone could ever give her. She was convinced you would say yes. She knows you pretty damn well, so I couldn't argue with her."

"Well, I'm always right!" Brandi says and walks over to us. She gives us both a hug simultaneously. "I love you guys so much," she says and wipes a tear forming at the corner of her eye. "Now, let's get inside and eat the rest of the food," she demands.

"What? More food?" I ask, surprised.

"Yeah, I'm starving after all that dancing," Brandi says.

"Oh, okay…" I reply.

"You know us Asians, we never turn down a good meal," my dad mentions, and my mom nods in agreeance.

I look at my sleeping daughter, concerned I should get her into bed. "It's okay, Hunny," my mom says to me. "Your father doesn't mind holding our lovely granddaughter, and Genesis is allowed to stay out a little later than usual tonight."

I look at Brandi and reply, "All right. I'm down."

"Here, Eva," Brian says as he grabs my hand. "This was Grandma Rose's wedding ring."

"Yeah, she gave it to Brian like right after that day we went out for sushi!" Brandi shouts. "You know, that afternoon we tried on dresses."

"Apparently, she knew," Brian says. "My grandma called me up and told me I needed to come and pick up the ring my grandpa gave her. She kept cutting me off and wouldn't let me talk. She said I needed to keep it on hand for when the time is right."

My heart rapidly melts thinking of Grandma Rose's approval. "Oh, my gosh," I say. "Where is Grandma Rose?"

"Oh, she busted one too many dance moves and headed home for the night," Brandi says. "Everyone else has left too. It's just us now. So, can we hurry this up so I can get some food or what?"

"We can stop by to see Grandma Rose tomorrow," Brian tells me and then offers to take Genesis from my dad's arms. "Here, let me give you a little break, Mr. Gin."

My dad gives Genesis to Brian and says, "She's going to be in good hands now."

"Yes sir, she will be," Brian replies.

My dad has always wanted the best for me. I feel like he has known all along what type of man I should end up with. It didn't matter that my dad gave my boyfriends the cold shoulder when I was in high school. What matters is that my parents love the man who wants me to be his forever.

My parents, Brandi, Max, as well as Brian and me, sit around a table stuffing our bellies with leftover food from the reception. I look around at all the people that have filled my life with joy. Their conversation and laughter echo in the room. Brian places his hand on my lap. I look at my daughter lying on Brian's chest and lean over to kiss him on the cheek. As we are just about to finish up our afterparty meal, Brian whispers into my ear and says, "I can't wait to grow old with you."

I rub my palm along the side of Mr. Right's cheek and smile at him. "Me too," I reply.

I pop the last bite of food into my mouth, and now my plate is empty… and my heart is full.

The end

Thanks for reading my novel!

I would like to take the opportunity to thank you for your purchase. The support of each reader means everything to me. I hope you fell in love with Eva's story. If you enjoyed my novel, don't forget to leave a review. I would love to hear from you!

Keep in touch with me on social media—where you can learn more about giveaways, discounts, and future novels. I hope to chat with you soon!

Follow me on:

Facebook and Instagram @leahghermann

www.ingramcontent.com/pod-product-compliance
Lightning Source LLC
Chambersburg PA
CBHW021143190726
48288CB00008B/2794
9781737967712